A Dream of Blood

WARRIORS OF THE OLD GODS

RHIANNON FUTCH

FUTCH AROUND AND FALL IN LOVE

Contents

Chapter One

Matthew

This café is almost too crowded for me to work. One table left in the entire place, and that's because it is next to me. The angry-looking man with little patience, a lot of tattoos, and no fucks to give about being nice to these people. Five people have come to the table next to me, looked over at me and left the building entirely. I'm going to have to tip all the barista before I leave, but it's worth it to keep a little distance. I hate getting to know them and then watching their short life spans end before I realize that fifty or sixty years have passed. I hate it even more because it reminds me she is still gone.

Its been so long since she died. The gods must have lied to convince me to do their bidding. Someone sits at my table and I look up to find one of the damned liars before me. "Hello Odin, what has drawn you here to bother me today?"

He raises a brow at me. "You know I can crush you with a thought. Why do you tempt me?"

"Because it has been hundreds of years and still not so much as a whisper of her. I would be content to join her wherever she may be now."

The old one-eyed bastard laughs at me. He places his hand flat on the table and a file appears under it. He slides it over to me and, withdrawing his hand, leans back to sit with his arms folded across his chest. "Your next target."

Opening the file, I scan the contents. Local priest. Church not far from here. The picture shows an older man with a plain face. According to the file, he is working on a high profile project that they want more information about. Just seeing the guy makes my stomach rumble. It's been a month since my last feeding, and I can't drink just any blood. No. The gods decided to be helpful and make sure I only crave the tainted blood of desecrated priests. "I'll take care of him."

"We want you to keep him alive long enough to find out what they are doing. We are hearing rumblings and none of it good."

The timbre of his voice changed, and I study him. He is truly bothered by this one. What the fuck is this guy into that is bothering the gods? "What kind of rumblings?"

He shakes his head. "We don't want to influence your search. It's better if you draw your own conclusions."

I can't stop my eyes from rolling at that. "Fine, but it would be a lot faster to find if I knew what I was trying to find."

He nods and stands. "We prefer thorough over speedy. One of us will check in with you soon."

I watch him walk out of the café. The bastard grins at me as he passes the window. I can't imagine why. I hear the bell over the door go off again, but I ignore it. What could have them so wound up about this guy that they won't tell me what I'm looking for?

That scent. Roses, patchouli, and musk, her scent. I search for the source as soon as I can force my eyes open and out of memories of the past. There she is. Her eyes meet mine and she smiles before turning to place her order. It's her. I could see it in her eyes. My love is back. Finally, my chance to win her love has arrived. Oh, I could cry with the relief at seeing her. At smelling that scent, that was her favorite even back then. Now I just have to try to not scare her into believing I am a lunatic.

* * *

Blaze

The café is really crowded today. Are they having a run on lattes? The minute I walk in my eyes and the fire inside are drawn to him. It's only muscle memory and the barista greeting me that save me from making a smiling fool of myself. Good god, no man has the right to be so damn sexy. It's all I can do to get my order out without turning to stare at him and those broad shoulders of his. The fire inside is leaping and joyous, like it found something it lost long ago. Dark hair, blue eyes, it's like God made him knowing my weakness for a man like that. The Lord is testing me and I did not study. How am I supposed to not drool over this man? I am a good, god-fearing woman. I can act right. I have a boyfriend. This man is not for me, no matter how scrumptious he looks. No matter that I somehow feel like I have missed him all my life. No matter that this fire inside, this destructive fire that would burn it all desperately wants to be near to him.

The barista passes me my latte and I turn to look for a table. Oh sweet Jesus, why is the only table in the place next to this tattooed man that I want to do terrible, sinful things with? Ok, Blaze, you can do this. You have a boyfriend. This is just another guy. I can do this. Besides, there is absolutely no reason why I should be so interested in this guy. It's just weird. Dear brain, act right for once, will you? It's bad enough the whole church thinks of me as the weird one.

Really, they only tolerate me because of James. Seating myself at the table, I do my best to ignore the man next to me while keeping my fire tamped down, so the chair doesn't start smoking. Pulling out my computer and setting myself to finding another mortuary hiring in the area is my distraction of choice today.

Chapter Two

MATTHEW

I have never been so grateful to be the scary-looking man that no one wants to sit near, since the only table left is the one next to me. Her scent is intoxicating this close. It looks like she is searching job boards. Is she a mortician? Or trying to get into the business? I need to find a way to break the ice with her. Working on my own research of the priest I've been assigned, I watch her as she works. She flips through tabs rapidly, flitting from one thing to another so fast I wonder if she has a touch of the supernatural this time. She knocks her cup off the table and my hand darts out to catch it before it spills more than a few drops.

She blushes, her cheeks going bright red as she thanks me.

"Always happy to help a gorgeous woman. Let me get some napkins. I'll clean those couple drops. The baristas here are really nice and I like to make their job a little easier where I can." It doesn't take long for me to collect a couple napkins and clean the small spill. Setting the napkins in my empty sandwich box, I look up just in time to catch her watching me.

Her cheeks are bright red again as she says, "Thank you, I'm sorry I'm such a klutz. I didn't mean to interrupt your work. I'll try to keep my latte to myself."

"I assure you, I am happy for the break. What brings you to sit in the café on such a lovely day?"

She looks at her screen for a moment, and turning back to me, she smiles ruefully. "I'm looking for another job. I don't think there is much chance for a promotion or even a raise where I work."

"And what do you do?"

She looks really nervous now, nibbling on her bottom lip. It's all I can do not to drag her into my lap and occupy that mouth with my own. She takes a breath and says, "I'm a mortician."

"Really? And you enjoy the job?"

Her face lights up as she tells me that helping to lay someone to rest has always felt really sacred to her. Plus, the bodies don't talk back. She goes on to say, "Sometimes it's almost like I get to help them to their final rest and I just really like that feeling, you know?"

"I can't say as I do. But I would love to hear all about it over dinner, perhaps?"

Her eyes round like saucers as she processes me asking her to have dinner with me. "I'm sorry, I-I can't. I have a boyfriend. I am really flattered and were I single, the answer would be a resounding yes."

I want to kill this man. No, I want to tear him into tiny little pieces for daring to look at her, but he has her in a relationship. He better be treating her well or I might actually kill him. "I'm sorry, I'm not usually so forward. I wouldn't have asked if I had known. He is a lucky man."

She shrugs. "If you ask our church, I'm the lucky one."

"Why would they believe something so dumb?"

"They like normal and, well, I'm not. I don't like the way people take such pleasure in other people not doing well. Then, being a woman working as a mortician. I don't wear enough damn light colored florals. You name it, I don't fit in. Really, I am lucky he even looked my way. I'm not conventionally attractive. I eat cake. My sense of humor is dark, and so is my reading list."

Her reading list?!? "What is your favorite book?"

Her cheeks flush with blood. Thank the gods she isn't a desecrated priest. Oddly enough, I still find myself suddenly hungry. "It is a series, really, but it's just too much. You don't want to know about it, really."

"I definitely want to know about a series that makes your cheeks so adorably red. I promise I won't make fun of you."

"How did you know?"

Now it's my turn to shrug and pretend everything is okay. Pretend that my temper didn't just rise to a killing rage. "It was a guess. You wouldn't be embarrassed if someone hadn't made fun of you about it at some point."

She grimaces and cringes, her shoulders folding inwards like she wants to make herself smaller, be unseen. I want to kill them all and wrap her in a blanket while feeding her tea and snacks, as she reads. "Yes, well, mostly they think the books are evil and that I'm opening myself up to it by reading them. But, the books are all about humanity and the ways the worst parts of it can infect everything and ruin a world. It's the Black Jewels series by Anne Bishop."

"I know that series, it's good. I can see the ideas that perhaps some people would be uncomfortable about, but the books are great. When books that challenge people on their ideas about what is good and right are labeled evil as a knee-jerk reaction, it gives me the ick about the people labeling it evil. So, what does your boyfriend do?"

"Oh, he is a deacon and the assistant to Pastor Ward. It's a very important job, though I'm not really clear on what exactly he does beyond the titles."

It can't be. "Pastor Ward? Of the Baptist Church of the Light?"

Her eyes widen and she nods. "Yes, how did you know?"

"My friend told me I should try that church when I get here, since I won't be able to go to my old one. He seemed to have a high opinion of Pastor Ward."

She shrugs. "He is a good pastor, I suppose. He always seemed a little creepy to me, but maybe I listen to entirely too many crime podcasts."

"I was going to start attending the church this Sunday. Is there any chance I could sit with you and your boyfriend, so I'll at least know one person?"

She smiles, and it's like the sun came out just for me. "Of course, I would love to introduce you to James and some of the others at the church. I'm sure they'll be thrilled to meet you and soon you'll be given the phone number of every single woman in the church."

She laughs and I think I could listen to it forever. "I think I'll pass on the phone numbers. I prefer to choose my own mate, and I'm a patient man." Her cheeks are bright red, indicating she understood what I meant. Good. "What time should I meet you there?"

"Hm? Oh! At the church! Yes. Um, it starts at nine am."

I can't help the smile that spreads slowly on my face. If she was even a little leaning towards breaking up with him already, I'd kiss the memory of him out of her mind. She isn't though, so I need to calm down. Some random guy walks up to her table and seats himself. She immediately asks, "What are you doing?"

The guy says, "My friend bet me that I couldn't get the number of the prettiest girl in here. I was hoping you'd help me prove him wrong."

I feel a deep need to intervene, but she looks mad, and I want to see what she does. I'll step in if she seems to want the help. Blaze closes her computer very gently and tells him, "How unfortunate for you. I don't give my number to strange men that think it's a good idea to sit at my table uninvited. Go play somewhere else, junior."

The guy's hands ball into fists, and he leans toward her across the table. "I don't lose bets and I always get the girl. Decide now how you want to do this, sweetheart."

Oh look, it's my cue. Her face pales with fear as his spittle flies at her. Standing, I grab his shirt and lift him off his feet as I walk to the door. He is immediately struggling and carrying on about wanting to be put down. I ignore him until we get outside. "What happened to how brave you were getting in the face of that woman? Is it only with people you think are weaker than you? That is my friend in there. You and your little friends need to forget she exists. If you see her walking toward you, cross the fucking street."

He sneers at me and tries to kick me, so I block his leg and punch him in the gut. Looking around, I think maybe I should take this into the alley where we can have an extended conversation away from all the passing cars and people. In the alley, I drop him. He crumples to the ground like a rag doll. Squatting next to him causes him to flinch. "Listen, son, I know you are trying to impress some fucking idiot friends you have. I want to point out that I carried you out of there while you struggled and carried on, but no one has come to check on you. Maybe rethink a few things when you catch your breath, eh? That lady in there is my friend, whether or not she ever becomes anything else, I will be watching over her from now until the day she leaves this world. If I catch you anywhere near her, I'm going to tear you into little pieces and scatter you about the city like confetti. Am I being clear enough here? Do we understand me?"

The guy has caught his breath and scrabbled back so he is up against the wall. "Yes, yes, I understand you. I won't go near her again. Please don't turn me into confetti."

His voice cracks a little on that last part. Poor guy. "Good! I'm glad we have an understanding. Now, let's get you up and dusted off. You can come back inside and apologize to the lady before you go on about your day. Somewhere else, right?" He takes one look at me and all the color drains from his face. I catch him before he hits the ground. What the hell? Oh, no! My damn teeth are out! They must have dropped with the protective feelings over her. Willing them back in, I realize, I don't even know her name yet. The guy is stirring, so I lightly tap his cheek after making sure my teeth are properly retracted. I don't crave regular blood, and I certainly don't need to bite people to protect her. His eyes round as he sees me. I smile at him and try to be a little friendly. "Hey, maybe you should see a doctor. You just up and passed out on me right when we were going in so you could apologize to the lady."

He nods excessively and works to right himself after thoroughly inspecting my smile. He is going to need therapy over this one. Returning to the café, he walks directly to her and apologizes profusely for his behavior, and promises it will never happen again. She is amused and forgives him. As I sit down at my table, she turns to me and says, "Thank you. You didn't have to do that, but I'm glad you did."

"I will always defend your honor." She looks confused, so

I smile and say, "Could I perhaps be graced with milady's name?"

"Oh! Yes! My name is Blaze. It's nice to meet you?"

Her hand is out to shake mine as I say, "Matthew. It's very nice to meet you, Blaze." The electricity when our hands touch, even in something so impersonal as a handshake, is stunning. Her face says she feels it too.

"I, um, I need to get to work. The dead wait for no one. Ha. I'll see you on Sunday?"

"You will definitely see me on Sunday, Blaze."

Chapter Three

MATTHEW

I can't help but be worried about how involved she might be in the church. What if she is part of what they are doing? Dread fills me as I pull into the parking lot of the church. The build is huge and looks to be based on baroque styling. The outside of the building is just dripping with scrollwork and molding. Even the windows have enough stained glass to build a commercial greenhouse. It certainly points to this church being involved in the things the gods are concerned about. Or maybe I am just jaded after so long hunting these fools. My eyes find Blaze standing at the end of the sidewalk, facing toward a wooded area off to the side of the building. No idea where the boyfriend is, maybe he wandered into the woods and was eaten by something. She is so lovely. Her blond hair is up today, little wisps sticking out all over. The gray dress hugs her curves down to her hips where it bells out. The heels are short. I hope they are just for church. Exiting the car, I make sure to close the door with more noise than necessary to announce my presence. It works. She looks over and smiles when she sees me. She smiled when she saw me. My heart is exploding with joy right up to the moment when he walks up and puts an arm around her. It's work to keep the smile pasted on my face when all I want to do is rip that arm off and beat him to death with it. Instead, I keep that smile pasted on and walk over to them. I thrust my hand out toward him as I say, "Hello! My name is Matthew. I am eager to find a new church to join, as I have only recently moved here. Blaze told me that this one is the best in the area."

He grits his teeth and pinches her side hard enough that she bites her lip as he shakes my hand. "We are always happy to add another sheep to our flock. Good to meet you Matthew! You'll sit with us today, but once you start attending on your own, the only unclaimed pews are toward the back currently. Don't worry, you won't miss out on anything there. We have a great sound system set up so that the sermon is heard throughout the church."

"That sounds fantastic, much like the church I went to in my hometown."

"Yes. Well, let's get everyone inside now. Come along Bea."

"Bea? I thought your name was Blaze?"

Of course he answers. "Oh, it is. But it's just such a ridiculous name that we've all taken to calling her Bea. It really works better for the congregation as a whole."

He pulls her along toward the doors to the church and I am just amazed. Changing her name entirely is better for the congregation? As I walk along behind them, I can see him whispering furiously in her ear. And I know it's better if I don't hear whatever he is saying. I need to bide my time. I want her with me more than anything, except her happiness. If being with someone else makes her happy, I'll support it.

But it sure as hell won't be this fuckhead. As we walk in there are five older women standing in the entry, they gush over the guy. Sounds like his name is James. Apparently, he gets to have his name because it is mediocre enough to suit everyone.

He removes his arm from around Blaze and tells her to find their pew while he escorts the ladies to their seats. She nods and turns to me. "Let's go sit, ok?"

I nod and follow her to the assigned pew. It is the third from the front and on the left. She steps in and over a space, leaving room for me next to the aisle. As I sit, she says, "No, you are supposed to sit on the other side."

Looking at her, I ask, "Why?"

"Because that is where James would sit if he came to sit with us."

"If? He doesn't usually sit with you?"

"Well, no, but--,"

"Then it will be fine, Blaze. James shouldn't have any problem with me sitting here. Unless you are worried he will be angry? Does he get angry at you a lot?"

She looks away. I hate him. She doesn't look at me at all as she speaks. "Maybe a little. He is kind of jealous. I don't understand it. I'm certainly no prize. Anyone here will tell you that. It's no big deal though, really."

She turns those big, green eyes on me with the last sentence. Those eyes begging me to let it go, to not say anything. So I nod and give her what she is silently asking. "I am here if that should ever change, Blaze."

We grab hymnals from the back of the pew in front of us and stand as the pastor announces we are going to start with a song.

. . .

* * *

Blaze

I just know James is going to be mad for a week over Matthew sitting in his seat. There is nothing for it, though. He's already sat there and if he asks questions... James is going to be really mad and no one needs that. I still don't know what set him off this morning. He knew that Matthew was coming. Knew that we were supposed to be outside when he arrived. My side still aches from that vicious pinch. It's going to be such a bruise.

And here is Matthew, being so sweet. The flames in me want to sing with joy, or at least they did when he arrived. Right now, they are an inferno I am still struggling to contain after James hurt me and said those terrible things. I know Matthew can tell things aren't right, but he dropped it just because I asked him to. And that just makes it worse because all I want to do is run away with him. When he arrived, my heart leapt with joy. I've never felt that way about James. He always scared me just a little, and if I'm honest, I think that is what he likes about me.

Looking at Matthew from under my lashes as we sing, I know we can't be friends. The man is singing a hymn, and it's the sexiest thing I think I have ever seen. The flames, I can feel them seeking a way out of the box I put them in. They don't like anyone in here except Matthew. I've got to stay away from him. The way I feel is wrong. I'm with James. Who am I kidding? I don't deserve to be with him, either. I need to break up with him and just stay away from the both of them. Oh God, what is James going to do if I break up with him?

The hymn ends and we sit. I can feel James glaring at me through the entire sermon. My heart is beating a million miles a minute. Even the flames have quit trying to break out, wary of what is to come. As soon as the sermon ends and we all file out of our pews, James is there almost immediately, dragging me back through the pew over to the far side of the church.

"What the fuck do you think you're doing? How dare you let him sit in my spot? Is that what you want? You want him to take my place? Is it? Is it?"

His voice is carrying across the now silent church. I can feel the heat of my blush. "James, I don't know what you're talking about, but you're making a scene. Everyone is watching." He looks around like he had forgotten anyone else was in the room. Then he grabs my hand and drags me out the side door into the parking lot. "James, let go of me. I don't know what's gotten into you, but I don't want to do this anymore. You can't treat me like this. I didn't do anything wrong."

He stops halfway through the lot and starts yelling at me again. "Of course you would pretend you don't know what you did! Do you think I can't tell you brought your fucking lover to the church? How fucking blind do you think I am?"

I am horrified by how on the mark he is for what I want, even if I can never have it. "James, you're talking crazy. I literally met him in a café and the second time I saw him was here at the church. You can't do this anymore. I just can't, I can't deal with your mood swings and the way you yell at me. James, we're through. I'm sorry. I just can't be with you anymore." It takes a moment for what happened to register. I am holding my face and looking away from James as I realize he hit me. He slapped me so hard. The side of my face is lit up with pain as he yells that we aren't through till he says we're through. A cold fire runs through my veins and I straighten. My hand comes away from my face and I see a little blood on it. Looking up at him, I tell him again, "We are through, James."

He lifts his hand and I brace myself for the hit, praying that I can keep the flames contained.

22

Chapter Four

MATTHEW

Can't run. I can't run to her without revealing that I am not just human anymore. I can hear him shouting at her as I push my way through all these fucking idiots trying to distract me from interfering. But he didn't drag her outside to talk to her. I know this as well as I know my own name, though I don't use Montamore very often. The doors are blocked by a group of women. As I get to them, they smile and preen and try to keep my attention. "Excuse me ladies, I think I left the lights on in my car." They seem put out as I push through with the lame excuse, but I don't care.

They should all be glad I am restraining myself.

All I want to do is tear his fucking head off for ever having touched her. The pinch earlier had me drinking my own blood because my teeth sliced my lips. As I get to the end of the sidewalk, I spot them, just as his hand connects with her face. All I can see is red as I jog over. I can hear the others behind me. The frustration of their presence has me grinding my teeth. She tells him they are over and he raises his hand again. I can't help myself. I sprint over. Grabbing his hand as it swings for her face a second time as he shouts, "A woman should learn in quietness and full submission!"

"Timothy was a misogynist asshole and not someone to admire or quote. We don't hit women."

Blaze opens her eyes and tears up at seeing I stopped him. James snatches his arm away from me and I let him. He sees the rest of the churchgoers behind me and moves closer to Blaze as he says, "What kind of man attacks a couple having a disagreement?"

Blaze steps away from him. "No, James, you hit me, not him. You attacked me. We are done, finished. There is no more us, not ever again."

"Would you like a ride home or to the hospital? That eye is pretty swollen." I reach out toward her face and James throws himself to the ground, screaming. We both look at him and he shouts about me, saying I shoved him. With a shrug, I look back at Blaze. "So, about that ride?"

She nods. "Yes, just get me out of here. I can't face everyone right now."

Walking her to my car, I can hear the other churchgoers fawning over him. What the hell is wrong with them? They literally watched him throw himself to the ground after he was caught hitting her and they are over there clucking about him like he is the victim. Getting her in the car, I jog over to the driver's side and get in myself. I see him watching us as I drive away. Asshole. I hope he is involved in the church really heavily.

"So, where to? I can take you to your home or the hospital or just anywhere you want to go."

She stares out the window. "I can't go home right now. Someone, probably multiple someones, are going to come to the house to tell me how terrible I am. I don't need a hospital or the bill that would come with some asshole in a white coat telling me that I should ice it and it will be fine in a couple weeks. Or the judgement when I decline to file a report with police that will definitely think it is my fault and that I should stop wasting their time. Thanks, but pass on that. It would be great if you could drive us around for a while and then drop me off back at my car. Or maybe take me to get an ice pack. That would be nice."

"Hm, an ice pack? I think I know just the place." The place is a diner I go to as often as possible, they know me there. Better than most right now.

She is quiet for the rest of the trip. It is only when I steer the car into the dirt and gravel parking lot that she looks away from the scenery out the passenger window.

"Why are we here?"

"This is the best place I know of to find you an ice pack." And maybe a friend. "Come, let's go inside. I'll introduce you to Frankie."

I am over to open her door before she stops looking at the building. She gets out of the car slowly, as though the slap had aged her, made her more cautious about moving about in the world. In the diner, I lead her to a booth in the back corner. Within moments of sitting down, Frankie is at the table asking what she can get for us.

"Frankie, my um, my friend Blaze here could use a bag of ice for her face before anything else. If you would, please?"

"What?" She studies Blaze and turns back to me. "Have you taken to beating up women now? What happened to her?"

Blaze chuckles at that. "He didn't beat me up. He stopped my boyfriend from beating me up any further."

Frankie puts a hand over her heart. "I'm so glad to hear that. I thought I would have to bash him on the head with something. Oh, your poor face. Come, we'll get you fixed up.

You can come into the back and get some ice on it along with something to ease the pain."

Not being invited to go along with them, I content myself with watching them as they go to the back room. I don't have much experience in dealing with people and their emotions anymore. Well, I've seen a lot of fear. That one is more enjoyable in the right people. Speaking of, I need to research that pastor a bit more, Pastor Ward. His sermon today was impassioned regarding the ways women should behave. I often wonder how the women feel coming to church to hear the word of God and instead hearing an hour or two lecture on how they should behave. Maybe I'll ask Blaze, eventually? Someday when I know her better. Right now, I just need to keep reminding myself that just because I still love the soul that she is, doesn't mean the woman she became this time will love or even like me this time. I don't know what I will do if she hates me this time around. Well, no. I know what I'll do. Stalk her and do my best to keep her safe till she dies. Then force the Gods to release me from our deal, somehow. Pastor Ward has somehow remained spotless throughout his life, even though every single wife he has ever had has died after an extended illness.

An extended illness that isn't named anywhere, even on the wives' social media. I wonder what he used to poison them with. Fucking coward that he is. I can't wait to rip into that throat and drink deeply. It seems like months since I last fed and I am eager to feel sated once again.

Frankie and Blaze exit the back room and it makes me happy to see Blaze is smiling again. She is so fucking beautiful. Blaze catches me staring at the two of them and frowns. Frankie glares at me. What the hell?

They get to me and Frankie asks, "Why are you staring at us so mean? What's your problem today?"

"I didn't know I had a mean look on my face? Sorry, um, I was doing some research while you were gone and I am kind of hungry. I assure you, it isn't about you."

Blaze nods and I want to sigh with relief. She sits down, gently putting a bag of ice back on her cheek. Frankie is happy again. "What can I get you? Coffee? Tea? Don't try the meatloaf, there is nothing good about it. Ever. I would suggest the chicken fried steak. I don't understand why they call it that, but it's what's good today."

Blaze says she'll have that with a sweet tea and I tell Frankie that I want the same. Silence reigns at the table after Frankie departs. "How's your face feeling?"

She shrugs. "Better than it was. I guess mostly I just feel foolish now. And I don't have a church to attend anymore. There is no way they are going to let me live down the fact that I left with you."

"Wait, what? You left with me because he was an ass and then he hit you."

"Yeah, but that's my fault for bringing you."

"What kind of twisted fucking logic is that?"

She looks ashamed, and I know I should have shut my damn mouth about two sentences ago. Dammit. "Well, as far as the people there are concerned, he was justified in his behavior because I brought you. I know it doesn't make any sense, but this is how they think. The women would tell me, when the men were not present, that if I wanted you to attend the church with us, then I should have waited to have James invite you. By bringing him with me to the coffee shop so that he could be the one to invite you and thus maintain his pride. But, since I can't ever do that shit, I got a lot of lectures from the women and the pastor about how I should behave if I planned to be a wife one day."

There has to be something I can say that won't make me

an asshole about this… Fucked if I know what it is. "I, uh, I don't quite know what to say. I'm at a loss." Frankie comes over with our food and her own plate. She seats herself next to Blaze after setting our plates before us. "So, what did I miss?"

Blaze fills her in, and she is at least as incensed as I am about the whole mess. I can see it in her eyes. "Well, honey, people are entitled to have their opinions, no matter how wrong they are. What do you want to do now?"

Blaze frowns. "I don't really know. It was scary when I broke up with him. I know I can't go to that church anymore. But, I think my job will be safe. I'm the only mortician he has that doesn't have hours that they can't be on call. I guess just go on with my life and try to do better next time."

"Honey, what about your parents? Don't they go to that church, too?"

Blaze finishes chewing and says, "They don't actually live here. We don't really talk much since I told them I wasn't going to marry their friend's son because it would be a good match for me. He was awful and the idea of being intimate with him turned my stomach. That was the last straw for them. They said that if I couldn't be a good and obedient, Christian daughter that I could go see how I fared with those filthy thugs I ran with." She chuckles. "The filthy thugs were a group of girls that I met with regularly for studying. We hung out at the library. Super tough, that's definitely what we were."

Frankie shakes her head. "You deserve better than them, anyway. Maybe we should start a club, Gen X women that went no contact before it was ok. Wait, shit, I'm assuming you're my age. How old are you?"

"I turned forty-seven earlier this year. Pretty thoroughly

Gen X. Old enough that I should have half-grown children if I had gone along with the plan my parents had for me."

Frankie bumps Blaze's shoulder with her own. "Having kids in a relationship that is bad for you isn't the way to go. That's why I raised my boy as a single mom. His dad and I were fun, but we didn't have any business being together. Even as the children we were when we got pregnant, we knew that. Our parents, not so much."

I watch the two of them talking and I think I could watch them for days. Frankie is the image of the daughter I always pictured us having before... Blaze looks nothing like the woman she was back then, except her eyes. Those green eyes that I could fall into forever. Frankie has them, or close to them. They don't draw me in like Blaze's do. It's as close as I will ever get to a glimpse of what our life could have been. Of course, that's as long as I ignore the slight swelling of Blaze's cheek and the way her shoulders curve in a little right now, like she wants to fold in on herself.

I am really looking forward to killing that guy.

They finish lunch and exchange numbers. It warms my heart that I got to introduce them. Walking back out to my car, she is smiling. "Where to? I'll take you wherever you want to go."

"I think all I really want to do is go home. Go to my little house and sleep until tomorrow."

"Then that is where I will take you. But I kind of need the address first."

She laughs. "I guess you do. Here, you can have my phone number too. Frankie says you're ok, and she's known you a lot longer than I have, so I think I am pretty safe trusting you."

After collecting an address and the happy bonus of her phone number, the ride to her home is fast. She only lives twenty minutes from the diner Frankie works at. Her house is a little wood frame house, cute and tidy. I park in the drive and run over to open her door. She gets out of the car and looks around, nervous. "Hey, no worries, I'm not trying to come in and ravish you or something. You've been through a lot today. I won't say I'm not interested. That would be a big lie." She chuckles. "Even if you never return the interest, I am still going to be here as your friend. I can promise I won't take advantage of you and I will remain a good friend unless you tell me you want otherwise. For tonight, though, I'd like to at least wait in the doorway until you have verified there is no one in the house. And to clarify, I am trying to respect your boundaries and autonomy. What I actually want to do is check your house for people and then have you pack a bag so I can install you in one of the bedrooms in my house to know you are safe." She shivers and I don't know if it is me scaring her or a chill. She doesn't smell scared and I don't think it's cold…

"I would like it if you would go in and check for me. I, I trust you to do that."

She holds out the keys to her house. If it were possible for my heart to leap out of my chest and dance, it would be now that it happened. "Why don't you wait in the car with the doors locked until I get back?"

She nods and sits down in the car. I watch to make sure she hits the button to lock the doors. Once she is secure in the still running car, I walk up to her front door and inspect it before I touch it. It looks fairly easy to break into and I really don't like that. But it doesn't look like it has been tampered with, so I'll have to be content with that. Hopefully, church boy is too good for breaking and entering. As I walk into the house, I am hit with her scent. It permeates the house. Walking through the house, I stop and check each window, the closets, under the bed, even the pantry. Her house is tidy and a little dark. My love is a little goth if the amount of skulls and such decorating her house are any indication.

Exiting her house, I leave the door slightly open. She hits the unlock button and I open her door. "Everything good in there?"

"It is. I made sure your windows were all locked, checked all the hiding spaces and the back door. Here are your keys." she takes them from my hand. The tiniest contact of her skin with mine sends jolts of electricity racing through my body. "I'll walk you to your door and listen for the lock, then I will go home. You have my number. Call or message if you need anything. I don't care what time it is. I don't sleep much, anyway." Or really at all, but maybe it is early yet to talk about my weird vampire habits.

She nods. "I probably will not call you. I should be fine. If he shows up here, I just won't let him in, and I'll call the police if he tries to force his way in. I'll be fine."

I am not fine with this plan. I don't like it at all. Can't say that. It's her choice how to handle things. But I can call her early in the morning. "That sounds good. Mind if I call you in the morning?"

She laughs. "You don't trust the plan. Yes, you can call me in the morning."

Chapter Five

Something feels wrong. I haven't opened my eyes yet. I know it is morning and near the time I planned to wake up. But I would swear it feels like someone is in my house. This feeling is what pulled me out of a lovely dream about Matthew that I will tell no one about. I can't bear it much longer, though. The fire is frantic to escape. To burn the threat to ash. I can feel someone staring down at me. My skin is crawling, insides burning. I can't take it anymore and open my eyes, fully expecting to see a monster in the room with me. As my eyes focus on James standing before me, I wish fervently for the monster I imagined. "Wha — What are you doing in my house, James?"

He smiles and I suppress a bone deep shiver. "I came to apologize. I know we had a fight yesterday, but it's nothing we can't get past." His hand shoots out to grab mine and tug me out of bed. Stumbling along behind him is an exercise in focus, though I managed to grab my phone from the nightstand. My heart feels like it will beat right out of my chest. What is that smell? It's not smoke. I don't think I'm burning anything yet. James doesn't seem uncomfortable at all. Nope, all the discomfort is reserved for me. A bug buzzes in my face as we get to my living room. He is looking at me, this expectant grin on his face. Looking around the room, I see wild flowers everywhere. My front door is standing wide open. A bug crawls over my foot. I want to scream and kick the thing at the front door, but I don't dare.

"Uh, wow. All these flowers for me? James, you shouldn't have."

He grins. Oh, thank fuck, I got the answer right. "I couldn't let my best girl think that I would leave a rift between us. I know you won't do that again, and neither will I."

Well, he's right, but not how he thinks he is. "How did you get in here? Did I leave the front door unlocked?"

His smile flickers but returns as I make it a concern that I failed. "No, you did good, pumpkin. The front door was locked. The owner is a good friend of mine and he gave me the key after I explained to him how I needed to make things right. That fight was just a big misunderstanding, and he saw it so he completely understood."

The fire in me flares and for just a second I am terrified that I am going to raze this entire neighborhood. My phone rings, saving me, them. Distracting. I look at the screen and answer Matthew's call, "Hi Mom! So good to hear from you. How are you?"

"Is he there now?"

"Yes, I think I can come to lunch with you." I look over at James. "You don't have anything planned for me today, do you, James?"

He smiles in a way that I am certain is meant to be benevolent, but sends icy fingers dancing across my spine.

"You should go to lunch with your Mom. Get yourself a new dress for the appointment this evening with the pastor. You should talk to your mom about our wedding. It won't be long, now that we are doing the meeting with the pastor. I can't wait to see you in the white dress walking down the aisle to me."

Matthew has been silent all this time, but now he asks, "Do I need to come and get you?"

"No, Mom, I don't need you to pick me up. I'll see you at our favorite place in thirty minutes. Love you, Mom!" As I end the call, James demands to know where my favorite place to eat is. "Chili's, of course. I just love the food and the atmosphere there. So does mom."

He nods. "Well, let's go get you dressed. You want to be pretty for your lunch with mom." He leads the way back to my bedroom and I can feel the flames licking at the edges of my vision. I don't know what is more terrifying, him or the fire. He insists I wear a long skirt and a pink fitted shirt. I hate the shirt, and not just because he bought it for me. I never wear pink. It just isn't my preference, and that is why this is the first time I have ever worn this shirt. "Make sure you eat healthy and light while you are out. You don't want to be bloated when we meet with the pastor. Plus, you need to lose some weight for the wedding. Can't have a fat bride walking down the aisle!"

Just get dressed and get out of here. Keep the fire locked inside. You can do this. Finally, I am dressed and ready. As we walk out the door, I stop to lock the useless fucking lock.

"Let me drive you to get your car."

"Oh, no, sweetie. I should walk the couple blocks, work off lunch some before I get there."

"That is a great idea. I'll see you this evening. Don't forget to get yourself a pretty dress for our meeting."

I mumble something about how I'll remember and see him later. He gets in his car and drives away. I wave as he passes me, walking. Once he is out of sight, I hitch up my skirt and run through yards, making it to the church lot in record time. I scan the area for him as I get in the car.

My phone beeps to let me know an Apple tag is near. Fuck. I head for Chili's. I'll put it on someone else's car while I'm there. Chili's isn't far and I see a big guy park his bike and go inside. Oh, that's where I am putting the tag. With a note. Pulling in next to him, I get and start looking for the tag. Which I am still looking for when he walks up. I'll just ask him. "Hi, um, I'm sorry to bother you." He looks very confused and sets his bag on the seat of his bike, standing on the side farthest from me. But he does wait for me to finish. "This is really embarrassing, but my ex put an Apple tag on my car somewhere. We broke up yesterday when he hit me in the church parking lot. I woke up to find him in my house this morning."

The guy looks concerned. "Do you want to file a report? I can help you with a restraining order."

"Restraining order? Oh, no. Not yet." Definitely not telling this guy how much that tends to piss off abusers and escalate the violence. I know he is trying to help. Oddly, my fire is kind of chill around this guy. I don't get it. "No, I was hoping you would take the Apple tag with you?"

He laughs, "I would love to. I am heading to the station and I'll put it in a cell there. It will be fun. What's his name?"

"Oh. That is fantastic. Let me find it. I was still looking for it. His name is James." I continue my way around the car and the guy comes over, starts feeling around various areas of my car.

"My experience has been that they tend to put it

somewhere easy for them. They think you are never going to notice it. So they aren't real careful about hiding it."

"That sounds like James." We get to the back of the car and he checks the bumper, while I start feeling around where my tag is. The air tag falls out when I pull the bottom of my tag toward me.

The guy picks it up and laughs. "He put his name and number on the case. Look, I'm an officer. My name is Chad, which is real fucking unfortunate right now. But I was with you when you found it. If you later decide to get a restraining order on him, tell them I was with you. Here is my card." He pulls a wallet out and extracts a business card from it. Taking the card, I try to stuff it in my pocket, only to realize that I am wearing a stupid skirt I didn't want to wear.

"Thank you. I will keep it in my purse. For now, I really appreciate you taking that tag for me. I have to go and meet some friends before they both call your office to report me missing." My phone pings right then. It's Matthew. "And there they are. Thank you again."

He moves back to his bike and as I get in my car he says, "You call me anytime. If he is scaring you or you just think he is around, you call me."

"I will, thank you." I don't see any point in telling him that an officer is the last person I will call for help under most circumstances. Typing fast, I send a reply to Matthew and start my car. The drive to the diner should be short, but I take a longer route, making random turns in case anyone is following me. My anxiety is high today and when I left the Chili's, my fire started right back in with trying to get out. What is it about that guy that calms it down so much? Pulling into the parking lot of the diner, I see Matthew inside. He was watching for me. I feel a way about that, but I really can't afford to look at that real close right now. He is at my side as I exit the car.

"When you were late, I was so worried about you. Are you ok? What did he do? Want me to kill him for you?"

"What? Whoa, we aren't trying to kill anyone. Calm down. I'm fine. Really. It was awkward and scary, but I'm good. I promise."

Chapter Six

MATTHEW

She tells me what happened as we walk in. My fangs are trying to drop and I really can't afford to show them to anyone here. After we are seated at the table, I can't help myself. "What are your plans?"

She shrugs. "I called a locksmith on the way here. Beyond that, I need to clean all the bugs out of my house. Get rid of the flowers. It will be fine. I'll have to find a new place to live eventually, but it will do until I find another place since he won't be able to get a key from the owner."

I don't like it. But I can't pressure her into anything. "It sounds like you are being pretty proactive about this. I'm glad to hear it. What about the air tag, though? Isn't he just going to put another one on your car?"

"Oh jeez. I didn't even think about that. I don't know. Search my car daily and put them on other people's cars? I gave the one today to an officer. I could call him and just keep giving them to him."

"Is there anyway I can help?"

"You did help. Your phone call got me out of there.

Admittedly, I can't go home anytime soon because he is making plans for us to… erm, I may have neglected to mention this at first. But he set up some meeting with Pastor Ward and he wants me to go with him to talk about our marriage."

"What? You broke up with him yesterday."

"I did. He doesn't appear to be counting that. I decided this morning wasn't the time to try and convince him."

"I would be happy to convince him if you like, you just say the word."

"As sweet as the offer is, I would feel bad if you went to prison for me. You've already done so much and we just met a few days ago. I can't let you do more for me."

Or a lifetime ago. I wish I could tell her. I want to tell her. But I don't want her to run screaming away from me. "I understand. I don't like it, but I won't pressure you further. Maybe I'll call you later?"

She smiles. "Yeah, you can call me. For now, I need to get some food and be off to work. Is Frankie not working today?"

"No, she isn't. But the guy that is waiting tables today is good." I turn and wave at him. He comes out from behind the counter where he had been chatting and keeping an eye on us. He has our orders back out to us fast and with minimal talking. I suppose he can tell we are talking of serious things and doesn't want to interrupt. Or maybe he takes a do not disturb approach. How do I protect her when she doesn't know me well enough to trust me? I want to scoop her up and take her off to one of my homes. Spend the rest of our lives making sure she never has to worry about anything. She is more relaxed as she orders her breakfast. Her smile. I would choose this life again and again just for the chance to see it. She looks back at me and her cheeks turn a lovely shade of red. I start to smile at her, but the hunger hits me hard. It's a sharp pain. No one has come in. I know there aren't any desecrated holy men in here. Why am I so hungry right now? My stomach is cramping with the thirst, as I clutch it I open my eyes and see her looking at me with concern. "Matthew, are you ok? You look like you're in pain."

The scent of her hits me and the hunger flares. Oh no. No, no, no. It can't be. Shoving the hunger down, I force a close-lipped smile. "I'm just hungry, is all. I forgot to eat this morning. He'll bring my food out with yours. I'll be fine. My body has never handled being... hungry, very well."

She glances up and smiles, "Good thing our food is coming right now."

The server places our food on the table and is quickly gone again. The smell of the food covers the scent of her, helping me to keep the hunger at bay. We are quiet as I devour my food. All too soon, the food is gone and her scent permeates the air around me. She finishes her coffee and says, "I need to get to work. Are you sure you're ok? You look like you are in pain."

I want to smile at her for reassurance, but I am afraid that if I do, she'll see things humans shouldn't see. "I'm fine, really. Don't worry about me. Let me walk you to your car." I drop some cash on the table, making sure I leave plenty to include a sizable tip. Watching her walk ahead of me on the way out has teeth and cock trying to grow, and I don't know which battle is harder to fight. Before I lose control of the thirst, I avert my eyes. Plucking them out sounds painful and growing them back would likely suck the whole time.

Outside, the air is better. Easier to smell things other than her. Rolling my shoulders to ease the tension helps. She seems lighter than when she got here. This morning must have been terrifying. "So, you are going to work and then home later tonight? Are you going to have anyone with you?"

She shakes her head no. "I don't have people that would believe I need protection from James. Honestly, it will be fine. He is going to be so offended when I don't show up tonight that he is definitely going to go out and screw someone else to get back at me. I'm sure I won't see him ever again. Really, you don't have to worry about me."

"I think I do. How about this? You call me or message me tonight and let me know you are in your house safe, with a brand new key from the locksmith. And I'll call you in the morning to come have breakfast with me, ok?" And I'll drive by a little, but you probably don't need to know that part.

"I will. I don't want you to worry about me, so I will definitely call tonight. And I like food, so I'll be happy to come and have breakfast with you. Go ahead and call me when you wake up and I'll meet you up here."

Blaze

I can't believe how long today has been. So many people... And no one to help with them since five. It's fine. I'm home, just put the car in park and get into the house. Key. New key in the pocket of my purse. Ok, got it. I walk the few feet to my door and it seems like a mile. The key slides into the knob so smooth. Wild the things that a little money can buy. No matter that it was roughly seven hours of work to pay for this, I have a good solid door knob that locks and I am the only one with a key. I pull the key out and drop it in my purse as I open the door and walk in.

As I shut the door, something hits it hard, and it rebounds to hit me in the face. Dazed, I look up and see James. His face is red and angry. "I'll teach you better than to embarrass me like this!" His fists hit me over and over, even after I fall to the ground. He is still shouting at me, but I can't hear anything over the pain and the roaring of the fire trying to escape.

He stops hurting me. I don't know how long it went on. The only fight I had in me was saved for keeping the fire contained. I hear him talking and I focus on the words this time. "You better never embarrass me again. Get yourself together. I expect to see you tomorrow."

The door slams and tears burn my eyes. I was such a fucking fool to believe he would let me go without a fight. Oh god, everything hurts. What's that noise? My phone! Oh god, purse, where is my purse? I manage to open an eye and look around. It isn't far. Maybe I can drag myself over? I know I can't stand right now.

Just as I get within reach of the strap, the phone stops ringing. Someone knocks on my door. Oh, please let it be Matthew. I try to call out; the sound is barely audible to my ears. Swallowing, I try again. A low sound escapes my throat. I know no one is going to hear that. But the door opens anyway, and he is there. Matthew, oh thank god he is here. I know he'll help me. Even the fire calms down, for now.

He is crying, murmuring softly as he grabs my purse and then picks me up. He is so gentle but oh god; it hurts so much. Then the world goes blissfully black, and the pain recedes into nothing.

Chapter Seven

Matthew

They've been working on her for hours. Finally, they are wheeling her into a room. She seems to be conscious. As I head for her room, a nurse steps in front of me, blocking my path.

"Sir, you can't go in there."

I don't understand until I look at her face. Oh, she thinks I did this. "I realize I am covered in her blood and I know what that looks like. I promise you, I found her like this. Have a look at my hands, feel free to inspect them all you wish. I didn't do this to her."

The nurse is thoroughly inspecting my hands when the doctor walks up. "What is your name?"

"Matthew de Montamore."

"Nurse, let him pass. She said her boyfriend did this and that isn't the name she gave as the boyfriend. She asked for this one. Say, did she happen to give you his last name?"

"No, she didn't. But his last name is Dunning. Why?"

"She doesn't want to press charges, but if she ever changes her mind, I like to have the full name."

I nod, not at all surprised. "Maybe I can convince her to press charges." Or I could bury him in the earth in a spot where no one will hear his screams.

He shrugs. "I wish you luck. If you hadn't found her, she would likely be dead by now. I just hope she isn't going back to him."

"He did this because she broke up with him. She isn't going back."

"That is a relief. I see so many that go back for one reason or another. It breaks my heart."

"Excuse me, I'm going to go in there now. I've been waiting to see her all this time."

He nods as I walk past him. I hear the nurse telling him that I might be the reason she got beat up and maybe I shouldn't let him in there with her. What if her boyfriend shows up? The doctor says something, but I am closing the door to her room and I miss it. As I round the corner, I see her poor face. She is shades of bruise and blood everywhere that isn't bandages.

"I'm okay Matthew. Well, sort of. I'm on the mend."

Shaking my head no, I walk over to the chair near her bed and move it closer. As I sit, I try to steel myself. Wait, I am not feeling the thirst now? I'm glad for it, but I don't understand why it affected me so much earlier and not at all now. Perhaps it is to do with the state she is in? "I know you are still just coming out of things, but I have to ask. Are you willing to move now?"

She looks away for a moment. "I will move, but I am going to do this myself. You aren't putting me in a house. I don't want to be dependent on anyone. Fuck, I wasn't even relying on James and look at what he did. I will move, but it has to be on my terms."

"I understand. I want you out of that house now, but I can exercise some patience until you are."

She chuckles and then groans, clutching her ribs. "They said my ribs aren't broken, but they are heavily bruised. I need to thank you for showing up when you did. They said the cut on my head wasn't clotting and neither were any of the others. I would have bled to death if you hadn't come to check on me. I am really grateful that I met you."

"I am really glad I could be there. The world would be a darker place without you."

The nurse walks in, "Visiting hours are over. You need to leave."

Blaze looks at me, her eyes wide and the scent of fear on her. I can't leave her alone. "Give me a moment, please."

The nurse frowns. "I want you out by the time I come back through with medications. Don't make me tell you again. I will have security ban you from the building." The door swings closed behind her, silent. I think she would have slammed it if she could.

Blaze whispers, "I don't want to be alone here."

Pulling out my phone and opening the contacts page, I find the folder with the board members' numbers in it. Choosing the one without children, I call him. He answers immediately, "Matthew! How are you? I haven't heard from you since the last board meeting. Everything ok?"

"Well, not exactly. That's what I called you about." It doesn't take long to explain the situation, and he fully understands my reluctance to leave her alone. He told me to sit tight and if the nurse came in before he arrived, to tell her that he is coming.

"I cannot thank you enough. I'll see you in five then."

The nurse walks in just as I finish the call. "I told you not to be here when I return."

"I know, but if you'll wait five minutes, Shawn Lake will be here and we can get all this worked out."

"Absolutely not. You are not staying with this woman. I know who you are! You are the guy that ruined her relationship and made a huge scene at church. That is James' fiancé and you are just some interloper. You shouldn't have been allowed in here to begin with!"

Blaze touches my arm. I look down at her as she says, "Sarah, are you serious? James is the one that did this to me. If Matthew hadn't found me, I would have died."

Sarah scowls at Blaze, and I want to throw her out the window. "James wouldn't have needed to do that if you hadn't been so willful. All you had to do was show up and talk to the pastor with him, get the pre-marital appointment out of the way. He already forgave you for meeting with this guy in secret. You should have been grateful."

Blaze's jaw has dropped, and she is just staring in horror at Sarah. "Listen, Sarah, right? You aren't a safe person to be around Blaze right now. That was incredibly inappropriate and, oh, look, there is Shawn now."

"Sarah, I would like a word with you in the hall, please. Matthew, I'll come see you soon."

Seating myself, I take Blaze's hand and tell her, "I'll be here until you leave. Get some rest. We'll talk quietly when Shawn gets back. He is going to make sure no one else bothers you with shit like Sarah said."

She lays her head down on the pillow and is sleeping within seconds. Shawn comes in a little later. I pull my hand away from hers, but before I can, her hand tightens on mine. I can't say it doesn't make my heart sing for her to do that, so I keep my ass planted in the chair and motion for him to come closer.

He lifts a chair and sets it near me, leaning forward to speak quietly. "What happened to her?"

I tell him the little I know, and he nods. "I heard what Sarah said. She doesn't work here any longer. She is a lawsuit waiting to happen. You are welcome to stay here as long as you like. I have told the staff to pass the word on that you own the building and you can be here as long as you like. The only ask I have of you is that you get out of the way if there is need. Having looked at her chart, I think the probability of that is slim to none." He glances over at Blaze and, seeing she appears to still be sleeping, he says, "She doesn't actually have insurance, so we have comped her bill. We are going to blame it on the poor behavior of Sarah. It helps us with the cause of her being fired, we won't be paying her unemployment. You can let her know when she wakes up that she will not have any bill from this. The hospital is paying the doctors and if any bill from this shows up in her mail, she should bring it directly to me. You give her my number. If calling is more than she can do right then, she can text."

"Thank you. I appreciate everything you have done. I did not know when I called you that it was going to go so wrong with the nurse. Honestly, I just wanted to stay with her in case he shows up."

"I understand. I think you and her should know, the policy here is to call the police in any time there is an assault. While they aren't fast to arrive, they will send someone. She should expect to see an officer here tomorrow before she leaves. She isn't required to file a report, but they are going to push for it."

"I understand. And I know she will understand why the hospital does it, but I think she is not going to file. Her faith in the police is not great."

"I understand. I am going to go and leave you to your

night in a chair while I spend the evening making up with a beautiful lady who was gracious and understanding about cutting our date short and has been waiting all this time in the car."

We hug briefly and he puts his chair back as he leaves the room.

* * *

Blaze

Waking up in the hospital is never good. I woke up in pain and confused for a brief moment until my brain kicked in and I remembered everything. Matthew is still here, and I was still clutching his hand when I opened my eyes. It was comforting, but I release his hand. I shouldn't lean on him so much. He smiles at me and asks how I slept.

"I guess I slept like the dead, because I was a little confused about waking up here at first. What happened with Sarah?"

"Sarah doesn't work here any longer. The hospital has taken care of your entire bill as an apology." Holy shit. Who the fuck does Matthew know with the power to arrange that? He continues after I manage to close my mouth as it fell open when he said my bill was taken care of. "Shawn is on the board here at the hospital and he actually heard what Sarah said, so he took care of things. He also wanted you to know that you are to contact him if you receive any sort of bill from this. I'll give you his number later. He also said that it is hospital policy to notify the authorities when there is an assault. An officer should be by here today."

Just what I need. Some jerk in a uniform trying to push me into pressing charges. "I guess I can listen to them before I tell them to go away."

He chuckles. "I thought you might feel that way."

"Have they said anything about when I will be released?"

"No, but I'm sure a doctor will be by soon."

That is the least satisfying answer he has given. Thank god the fire is staying banked. It's almost like it is giving me time to recover before we continue our fight.

There is a tap on the door and an officer walks in. "Hello ma—, it's you. Was this done by the same guy that put the tracker on your car?"

Matthew looks at me with a raised brow, and I feel heat rushing to my cheeks. I didn't expect the officer to be the one from yesterday. My fire is oddly comforted by his presence though, like I don't think I even need to hold it back right now. "Hi, um, yes. It was. He ambushed me at my house last night."

Chad frowns. "Is there any chance you would be willing to press charges against him?"

"He did this because I didn't show up to a marriage appointment he set. I don't want to think about what would happen if he found out I talked to you."

"How about this? I will do an interview with you. You don't have to press charges. But this will create a paper trail. It will provide some sort of evidence if you have to go the route of putting him behind bars. It will show a pattern of violence that will help your case. And I just won't turn it in unless you give me permission."

I want to trust him. He feels like I should trust him. "And you won't contact him about it? He won't have to know? You promise me that this won't go into the system unless I give you permission?"

"I promise. If I have it written down, then I can take the hassle for having 'lost' it for a little while. My boss will understand once I explain it."

Everything in me feels like I have to trust him. I don't get it. I'm not attracted to him at all, but I feel this closeness, like

I have known him all my life. He is the definition of conventionally attractive. Tall, muscles for days, blond, and a friendly wolf sort of personality. I don't understand it. "Ok. I'll trust you this one time. Because you feel like family. Make sure you don't get me killed with this."

He looks surprised and says, "You feel it too? I noticed it yesterday but chalked it up to insanity. Who are your parents? My mom was a teen mom, and she gave me to my father's family because her parents were not ok with it."

"My mom is Mary Mowlen. Her maiden name is Smythe."

His eyes get really round at that. "I think maybe we need to get a blood test. That is my mother's name. That is a fairly common name, though. Maybe it's a coincidence. For now, let's get this form filled out. I'll lose it in my car until you say otherwise."

Matthew, who has been quiet and watchful this entire time, stands and says, "I'm going to step out for a minute and ask some questions about where we could get a dna test done fast." He lifts my hand to his lips and places a gentle kiss on my knuckles. "I'll return quickly. Officer, will you stay until I return?"

"You can call me Chad, and yes, I will."

I tell Chad the whole stupid story, shame burning my every pore, because I let it get to this point before I even noticed that things were bad. After I finish, he says, "Listen, I know you probably feel like you are to blame for things, but I need you to know it isn't your fault. Maybe you see things now that you think should have been a sign, but you wouldn't have known that then. And more importantly, his behavior is on him. You are not responsible for anyone's actions, but your own."

To say I wasn't expecting that would be understating it

more than a little. All anyone at the church ever said is that it is all my fault if he flew off the handle and behaved irrationally. I feel tears burning my eyes and I swipe at them before they can escape. "Thank you. I, I needed to hear that. So, how long have you been a cop?"

He chuckles. "Not long enough for the shine to wear off my badge. It took me a while to decide what I wanted to do. But my size allowed me to be a bouncer, so I did that to pay bills while I tried things. I still do it, but it is more of a side job now."

"Oh? What bar?"

"The Celestial Oddfellows. It's fairly chill, but they employ us to make sure it stays that way."

"I've heard of that place. Didn't someone die there a couple of months ago?"

His brows reach for his hairline as he says, "Yes. How did you know?"

"I am a mortician. I wasn't the one that collected the body, but I was the one that it was brought to. Since they knew how she died, they didn't feel the need to autopsy her."

"Oh! Well, that's kind of cool. Do you like your job?"

"The job itself, yes. My boss, not so much. I've been looking for a different place to work, but no luck yet." Matthew comes back in then, two people following behind him.

"Sorry to interrupt, but these two were here delivering some other results when I was asking about dna testing. I got you bumped to the front of the line and got some collection supplies from the hospital. So, if you want to know, you can in a couple of days." He gives Chad a strange look that I don't understand as he says, "Don't worry, they're safe." The two attendants' eyes flash strangely, but it's gone so fast I can't be sure I really saw it.

The tension that had tightened Chad's shoulders when Matthew said he got us bumped to the front of the line seems to melt away as he says they are safe. What the fuck is going on there? Before I can ask, the attendants are taking blood from each of us. They are fast and efficient. It's done, and they are gone almost as quickly as their eyes flashed. I don't think I even heard them speak. So weird, aren't they supposed to do permissions and make us sign things about this? Chad seems fine with it though... Maybe it's just different because Matthew is having it done privately? Matthew and Chad are talking quietly over by the tv so I can't hear anything they are saying. But the doctor comes in and asks how I'm feeling.

"Aside from the aches and pains you said would be there, pretty good."

We go through the whole checkup and thank fuck Matthew and Chad stepped out for that. The doctor was just ignoring them. This place is fucking weird. The attendants that take blood and no forms to sign, a doctor that ignores two men in the room and has odd tests. Why does he want to know about my usual temperature perception? What does that have to do with anything? "So, am I getting discharged now?"

The doctor looks up from where he is inspecting my hand thoroughly. More fucking weird shit. My hand isn't injured. "Oh, yes. We'll have you out within the hour. I think I have everything I need now. I'll go sign the papers for you to leave. A nurse should be by soon with the discharge papers. If you should have a strange fever soon, don't hesitate to call my office. They'll put you through to my cell immediately." He hands me a card and gives me a very intense look. "Promise me you will call if you have a sudden, strange fever."

"Um, sure. Is there a concern about an infection?"

He starts to speak, stops, and says, "There is a possibility of a very specific side-effect. That's all. You should have nothing to worry about, but just in case, keep my number in your phone."

"Ok. Will do, doc." He leaves and since he said I'll be out within the hour, I get out of bed and pick up my clothes. They are bloody all over. I don't want to wear this out of here. People are going to try to put me back in. I wonder if there are some clothes in the lost and found that I could wear home? Matthew comes in then with a bag and I hurry to close the back of the gown I'm wearing. Man, hospital clothes are a fucking danger to the modesty.

He grins at my hasty clutching of the gown. "I thought you might be hesitant to put that clothing on, so I sent out for something not covered in blood. It's just sweats, but I think they will fit you and not be too bad if I was wrong on the size a little."

"Holy fuck, thank you so much. You have saved me once again. I was about to ask the nurses for something from the lost and found."

He laughs, "Yeah, covered in blood is not a great look for leaving the hospital. I'll be out here with Chad. Just open the door when you are done. Unless, do you need help?"

Well, that didn't occur to me either. "I don't actually know. I'll shout if I do, ok?"

He nods and leaves the room. Here's hoping I don't need help. I can do this. I can definitely do this. Reaching up isn't too bad and I get the hospital gown off easily. The sweatshirt goes on pretty easy too, not the least painful thing ever, but manageable. The pant however, are a whole other issue. Apparently the bruises on my ribs like the idea of me bending about as much as they like the idea of being deeply pained and passing that agony on to my entire body, causing me to drop the pants I was trying to put on. Carefully crouching down while holding my torso very straight, I grab the pants and stand up. That was damned exhausting. Walking back over to the bed, I ease myself back up onto the mattress. Pulling the blanket over the goodies, I resign myself to help putting on pants. Along with the fact that I don't even have panties to help with the modesty thing. My cheeks must be bright like the sun, because they certainly feel hot. "Matthew," I call out and he opens the door immediately. "I need a little help."

He crosses the room, looking at me curiously until he sees my bare legs hanging out from under the blanket I have pulled across my lap. "Oh."

"Yes. Oh, indeed. So, I was thinking, maybe you could put these on my legs and push them up to my thighs, then just kind of hold them up while I slide into them as I stand? I don't think I'm explaining this clearly. Please tell me you understand what I mean?"

He nods. "I do." He takes the pants from me and gently slips them on one foot. Holy hell. How is this turning me on? What the fuck is wrong with me that his sliding pants up my legs is making me incredibly needy? If it wouldn't hurt like hell, I would seriously think about asking him to pull them right back down. "Blaze." I snap back into focus and his face is right in front of mine. He looks as strained as I feel. "Blaze, slide forward so we can get these pants on you before I beg to pull them off you."

Oh. Oh my. "Um, yes. Indeed." Pushing my hips forward while I keep my hands braced on the bed is working except for one thing. As I slide down so my feet touch the ground, my pussy drags across the massive erection standing straight out from his body, causing him to groan. The material of the sweats may as well not even exist. His eyes are clamped shut, and he is biting his lip as I stand very still, his erection pressing into my belly now that my feet are on the ground. "Uh, Matthew."

"Yes?"

"I'm good now. Well, my pants are on."

His eyes fly open and he steps back quickly as his hands drop to cover his erection, "Sorry, sorry. I wasn't, um, hmm, I'm sorry."

"It's ok, really. I know they have a mind of their own and well, it was definitely, uh, distracting. But no worries and no apologies needed."

A knock sounds on the door, and the nurse opens the door immediately. "Oh good! You're dressed! Excellent. Let's get your discharge paperwork done and get you out of here." She breezes past us to the table at the end of the bed, starting the discharge spiel before I can even get over there. I guess she's used to no one really listening to the whole thing or any of it, really.

It doesn't take long for the discharge process to be completed. Which is kind of odd, but I'm not asking questions about it because I certainly don't want to wait five hours for them to get around to it. When I get wheeled out of the room, I see Chad is waiting. He asks the nurse if he can wheel me out. She shrugs and walks away. I wonder what this place is like if you don't have Matthew on your side? A shiver runs through me at the thought. Chad says, "Are you cold? Let's get you outside."

He doesn't wait for an answer, but as I think about it, I don't think I have ever been really cold in my life. I've always had this fire in me, keeping me warm and busy trying to contain it. I still have nightmares about the one time it slipped loose while I was a child. My mother lost her shit about it and when my father asked what happened, telling him that the fire in me escaped and I was so sorry was the last straw for her. She slapped my face, called me a liar, and sent me to my grandmother's house for a month. Grandma wasn't much better. She tried to do something that would make it go away, but my fire just burned right through it. I need to stop thinking about this. My fire has been so calm with Chad around, but thinking about the past just gets it riled and it wants to burn the shit out of everything. Outside, Chad parks the wheelchair and Matthew gives me his hand as I stand. Chad runs a hand across the back of his neck. "I feel weird asking this, but could I get your number?" He looks at Matthew. "I think I would like to exchange numbers with you as well, if you don't mind. Could you call me as soon as the results come in? I'd like to be there when we find out."

Matthew grins at him. "You can have my number. I think it's pretty certain the test will come back within the next couple of days and affirm what we already know." He touches his nose like that means something, and Chad nods like he understands the meaning. What the hell is up with this shit? I need to have a talk with them. Today is not that day. Tonight really. Tonight I just want to go to bed.

We do a number exchange and Chad leaves as he is on the clock and his speaker thing has been going off for a while. A car pulls up and the man driving it gets out. Matthew hands him some cash and opens the passenger door for me. "Is this your car?"

"One of them. I sent the other one to be cleaned. I wasn't terribly cautious about the upholstery." He shrugs with a rueful smile as he closes the door and goes to the driver's side.

"So, you are taking me to my house, right?"

He glances at me. "What? Why would I take you there?"

"Because that's where I live. I need to go get some sleep."

"You aren't safe there! I thought, or I assumed, you would let me take you anywhere else?"

"The only reason he got to me is because I was tired and not paying attention. That won't happen again. It'll be fine. You'll see. Take me to my house, please. I'll even let you come in and thoroughly check the place. You can stay the night on the couch if you really want to, but I want to go home, Matthew, please."

He growls, "You know I can't deny you anything! Fine. I'll take you home, but I am definitely staying there with you. I'm not leaving you alone there. Not while he is still out there."

Chapter Eight

BLAZE

We get to the house and it looks fine. I don't even see any blood on the walk. It's like nothing bad ever happened here. I don't expect it will be quite the same inside. We get out and Matthew insists that he go in the door first. I am fine with that, a few more seconds before I have to face the wreck of what James did. Matthew unlocks the door and pushes it open. Reaching in, he flips a switch to turn on the light. His body stiffens, and he snarls, "What are you doing in her house?"

Fear hits me, punching ice straight into my heart and making my fire go wild with the urge to burn everything, burn the world to ashes, so long as we are safe. Then I feel Matthew's hand reach back and take mine. The world comes back into focus. I feel safer knowing he is here with me. I peer around Matthew to see James looking confused until he spots me. Then he smiles and says, "Oh honey, what happened to you? Send your friend on home so we can talk about this."

The idea of Matthew leaving me alone with him has me

grabbing the back of Matthew's shirt. I whisper, "Please don't leave me alone with him." He gives the hand he is still holding a little squeeze to let me know he heard me. Raising my voice, I tell James, "He is not leaving. James, you shouldn't be here. I want you to leave."

"I'm not leaving. You are my fiancé, and I have every right to be here. He needs to leave."

Matthew lets go of my hand and I am terrified for a second that he is going to leave. Then he pulls his keys out of his pocket and says, "Blaze, why don't you go sit in my car with the doors locked while James and I have a little talk?"

I try to thank him, but the words are barely more than a little air passing through my mouth. He gives me a little pat, and I near run to his car. Inside it, I hit the button to lock all the doors and work on slowing my breathing as I calm the flames inside. I must have gotten lost in the dance to calm my flames, because next thing I know, Matthew is tapping on the window. I hit the button to unlock the doors, and he opens mine, crouching down to look me in the eye. "He is gone. He doesn't appear to have done anything except sit there and wait for you to come home. We talked about things. I think he may understand that you do not wish to continue the relationship. That doesn't seem to have improved his attitude about things and he is still quite certain that he should be allowed to speak with you. He is convinced that today is not that day."

I nod. "Good. Did - did he tell you how he got in?"

"He got a key from the owner for the back door."

"What? I don't even have a key for the back door!"

"And that is why I am begging you to let me take you somewhere else. Somewhere I can keep you safe. Where the shit guy you rent from can't give out keys to your place." He reaches out and takes my hands in his. "Please, let me keep you safe. Please."

"What are people going to say about me if I go away with you? Especially with James telling them how you brought me home."

"Those people are going to talk bad about you no matter what you do. They talked bad about you Sunday at the church. Those are not your people, you know that. You don't ever have to see them again."

"Where would you take me? I don't know…"

"I own a hotel. It's a big, fancy place. I have a suite and there is a second one next to mine. They don't have connecting doors or anything, it just made sense to put in a second one for that space. I rarely allow it to be used, usually only by friends passing through. You don't plan to stay, so you fit pretty solidly in that description. You could stay as long as you like, though. Hell, live there forever. I'm fine with it. Please let me do this for you."

Looking at the house, I swear I see someone move in the bushes. I watch for some time but I don't see anymore movement. Is that possibly where James hid when he ambushed me going in the house? "Ok. I'll let you put me in the spare suite. Jesus, how rich are you? No, don't answer that. I don't need to know. It doesn't matter. Let's go in and get the important things." As we walk in, I am grateful for the time I spent calming my flames. They are playing fairly nicely for now. It almost seemed like they were waiting for me to decide before they chose how they would behave. Inside, I grab a bag and toss it on the bed. Clothes, important papers, and some shoes get shoved in. When I try to pick it up, suddenly Matthew is there, lifting my bag and moving it right out of reach.

"I'll carry it for you. You are still healing. Is this all you need?"

"Yes." Looking around, I realize this place barely even looks like I live here, to me at least. I have things, little decorations, but not enough to fully make it mine. "Let's go. The rest isn't super important."

He leads the way out the front door and as I close it behind us, he asks, "Would it be all right if I send a moving company to put it all in storage for you?"

Pausing, my hand on the doorknob still, I want to say no. But the realist in my mind asks how I would manage to pick up a box when, truth be told, I was relieved that he picked up my bag before I could? "Yes. You can. I don't like it, but I realize I am not going to be in any shape to do it myself for a little while. So do the thing and I will try not to be cranky because I can't do it."

Chapter Nine

MATTHEW

Her face when she saw the suite I had for her was concerning. It never occurred to me that the amount of money I have could be a problem for her. I don't know how to fix that. I could give more away? As fast as it comes in now, I'm not sure I could keep up without making it a full time job. Perhaps I could find ways to do more? I don't know. Maybe I'm an asshole for not thinking of this before now. What if I opened a domestic violence shelter and funded it fully myself? Give women like her that don't have someone to defend them a place to go. Yes. I can't hide it from her, but maybe it won't be terrible if I omit why I had the idea?

That is a job for tomorrow. Tonight, I need guards outside her room, in case he somehow tracks her down. Because I have work to do.

An hour later, I am in the car on my way to Pastor Ward's house. I park at a trailhead not far away and stroll to his place. When I can see the lights through the bushes, I step into one as I phase into smoke. Slipping into his house is only a matter of finding a crack. My spot is at the back door. It doesn't fit the frame anymore, letting me slip in through the gap. Following the sound of voices, I find Pastor Ward and James in what appears to be a home office.

"James, what were you thinking? Leaving her there after the punishment? If you don't hold back, then you must deal with the consequences. From what Sarah said, she would have died if she hadn't been brought to the hospital."

"I didn't realize she was so bad off and I was furious about the way she humiliated me. Now she has run off somewhere with that Matthew and I don't know where to even start looking."

Pastor Ward walks over and pats James' shoulder. "Don't worry yourself about trying to find her. One of the flock will let you know where she is when they see her. The subliminal messaging in the music has been working wonderfully. The flock has more than doubled and tithes have grown with the flock. We'll have to expand the church soon. That need will be a fantastic way to get even more donations and volunteers. The plan is progressing and we'll be running everything soon enough."

James puts his head in his hands. "I agree that the messaging is working, but I don't like Bea bringing men to the church. Could I insist she wear earplugs so she isn't trying to bring in more people? I feel like it encourages her into bad thinking."

The pastor walks around the desk and seats himself. "Yes, earplugs for her will be acceptable. We'll put it about that she has been diagnosed with something and has to wear them because she is sensitive to sound. If we phrase it right, she will look even more weak and foolish to the rest of the congregation, keeping her isolated and in your home where she should be. You two should marry as soon as possible and start working on a family. Two or more children should keep her plenty occupied. And being married will reflect well on you."

James smiles and I want to go down there and rip his throat out so I can watch him drown in his own blood. I manage to stay in this form, but it's a fight. Holding tight to the memory of Odin saying that the pastor needs to live until we find out more of what they are doing is all that holds me in check. She is finally here. I can't fuck this up now that my chance has arrived. They move on to talking about the congregation and after a time I slip out, having gotten as much as I will tonight.

I make a stop at the church and steal one of their discs. The sound system is not recent. Getting back out is a little more challenging while keeping the disc, but I do it. It isn't likely that anyone will see the disc floating through the air, and if they do, they'll just think they are seeing things. Hopefully, this disc will help me find out who is creating it for them and get some changed messaging into the rotation. Once I find someone that can do that for me.

* * *

Blaze

It seems like I haven't been to work in a few weeks, but I'm pretty sure it has only been two days. Waking up in this place was a little disorienting, and it took me longer than usual to get myself together. But I am pretty sure that I haven't missed any days yet. Calling the office, I wait through multiple rings till he finally picks up. "Hi, it's Blaze. I was assaulted and while I am out of the hospital, I was told that I can't lift anything heavier than ten or twenty pounds for the next month."

"That isn't acceptable. You are going to need to pull your weight if you want to retain your employment here, young lady."

The fire inside me leaps to angry and ready to burn through the world. "Excuse me? Are you saying that you are going to fire me despite my doctor's note? Pretty sure that isn't legal."

"It doesn't matter if it is legal or not. This is an at will employment state and my will is that if you are unable to perform the duties of your job, I don't need you."

"You can't do that. What you can do is have me work at the reception desk until I am able to lift things again. Then you could have the phone answered in a timely fashion and stop losing business to places that answer their phone."

"All right, but I'm not paying mortician rates for front desk help. You get half time until you are back to mortician work."

"If you pay me half, I'm going to the Better Business Bureau. I'll see you this afternoon, Rick." Hanging up on him isn't nearly as satisfying in the age of cell phones. What I wouldn't do for one of the old corded phones, you could slam them down repeatedly until you hit the hang up by accident. It was a type of satisfaction that just doesn't exist anymore. I think that might have helped me to calm the flames, too. Instead, I get to do breath work and meditation.

I spend the next few hours slowly getting myself together to go back to work. Staring into the mirror, I kind of wish that I was a full-coverage makeup girlie. Unfortunately, I am a minimal makeup girlie and that is what I have to work with. So, minimal is getting more minimal. There is no way I am going to be putting eyeliner on. Mascara is fine, lip balm is good, and a lightly tinted moisturizer. That's all I got for today. Maybe Rick will be less of a jackass once he sees my face.

Either way, I need to work and I can deal with whatever stupid shit he has to dish out while I continue to search for another job. It kind of sucks that morticians tend to stay put at a job until they are in need of the services. It would make it a lot easier to find a different job if they quit a little more often.

I am thrilled that Matthew got my car here. Happy enough that I'm not going to ask how. Driving gives me way too much time to think about things like how it would be possible for me to have a brother. Did my mother really have a child before me and walk away from him? What happens if we are brother and sister? Do I tell my mom that I know her dirty little secret? What if he wants to meet her? How do I do that? Do I spring him on her like, surprise, I found my brother? Or tell her and let her have some say in it?

I mean, he is a cop. I don't guess he really needs me to find her. He could search her address and go find her. Why hasn't he in all this time? Maybe he doesn't care to meet her? Pulling into the parking lot is such a relief from the thoughts racing through my mind. Though, now that I am stopped, I realize even the thought of Chad has calmed my flames. I wonder if I can just use that all day?

Chapter Ten

Matthew

Finding people to work on the disc took the entire morning. I haven't seen Blaze yet, so I grab some food on the way back to the hotel. I get to our floor and as I head for her door; the guards tell me she left.

"Did she happen to say where she was going?"

"No, we didn't ask either. Do you want us to in the future?"

"No, I don't want to control her or spy on her. I just wondered if maybe she said in passing." Holding out the bag of food, I ask them, "Want some lunch? I am going back out." They are happy to accept the food and I tell them to get a few more guys so they can rotate shifts. I don't want anyone sneaking into her place. They nod and one pulls out his phone. I step back into the elevator, jabbing the button for the first floor and hoping James hasn't been by her work yet.

It is a long ride to the funeral home where she works. I've never seen the place till now. It's on the outskirts of town and has lost any pretense to chic, only the shabby remains. The shingles have moss growing over most of them. It won't be much longer before they need a new roof. The building itself is block and hasn't been cleaned for at least a decade if I had to guess. The gray of the building gets darker as the eye follows the line of the building to the ground. Once I have parked across the street in a shaded spot, I open the window just a little and slip out in the smoke form that serves me so well. The building she works in hasn't got a good seal anywhere, so getting in to check on her is a snap. She is at the front desk. I don't have to go far even. She looks like she has been crying, but is otherwise safe. Back out to my car before I decide to appear in there to find out who made her cry. Scaring her to death will not help the situation. I can stay here and make sure that James stays far away from her. It isn't stalking if I am here to protect her, right?

* * *

Blaze

Rick's attitude had not improved by the time I arrived. He didn't linger out front after telling me I look like shit, so there's that. As if I couldn't see that in the mirror this morning. My face is a mottled landscape of blues, yellows, and purples. The tinted moisturizer that I use covered some of it, but even full coverage isn't going to hide this without way more skill than I have at present.

By the time I am settled in at the front desk, our first client of the day has arrived. By the time Shelley is out here to take care of her, the phone is going off. Only two of the morning calls were shitty church people telling me what a terrible person I am. Thankfully, no one was out here for the one that made me cry.

I brought lunch with me and as drained as I feel; it was a good idea. The afternoon starts pretty well, if with a larger than average number of people having passed in a rather strange manner. I've never seen so many people with closed caskets because their throats were ripped out. It's almost like an animal has been running wild in the city.

Icy fingers of dread pierce my heart as I see two of the church women get out of a car. Fuck me. Susan is the first one in the door, and she smiles evilly when she sees me. "How dare you treat James like that? He is a good man and you are just the trash he seems to be stuck on. I'm telling you now, if you don't shape up, you are going to lose him and my daughter is finally going to have herself a good man."

Ethel continues the assault, saying, "Unless he takes a shine to my daughter. What were you thinking about, riling him up like that? Our job as women is to serve and be helpmeets for our men. You've done nothing but make his life miserable since he first laid eyes on you."

The flames are racing under my skin, begging for a way out. For me to let them burn, burn, burn. In a voice smaller than I intended, I tell them, "His violence isn't my fault. Your daughters can have him. I don't want him."

Susan laughs, "As if it is your choice! You should just be glad you are being given a second chance to make things right with him. You should be on your knees begging him for anything he will grant you. And you are nothing but trash. That's why no one has ever met your parents. I just know they disowned you years ago for being so damn weird." Her face is twisted with the malice she exudes as she says, "Oh, I struck a nerve, did I? Little girl needs to go cry but has no mommy to run to? You are weak! You shame all of us with your disgusting behavior! Imagine, taking up with a new man and bringing him to the church your fiancé is a deacon at? It makes me wonder about your parentage and if perhaps you just managed to out trash your parents."

The tears are flowing freely down my face now. Every poisonous word from her lips feeling like a needle stabbing my heart. "Think what you will, but you need to leave this place of business now or I will be forced to call the sheriff." Picking up the handset from its cradle, I dial the number to the sheriff's office. Putting the phone on speaker, I let them hear the dispatch answer the phone. They look at each other and beat feet to the door as I say hello. "I'm sorry to have bothered you. There were two women," I watch them jump back in the car and speed out of the parking lot. "In here harassing me and letting them hear you answer the phone convinced them it was time to leave."

We talk briefly, and she tells me to call the emergency line if they come back. I promise I will and hang up the phone. At this point, I think I need to go home for the day. I don't think I can handle much more. The flames are snapping and popping, looking for any reason to roar. My mind is made up as I head for Rick's office. His door is open and I walk in to find him watching wrestling. The sound is down really low, and he also has the security cameras pulled up, focused on the front reception area.

"Are you kidding me? You watched the whole thing, and you just let them attack me?" The flames are roaring in my ears. Clenching my fists helps to keep them in, but I don't know for how long.

He shrugs. "They weren't saying anything about the business, and there weren't any other clients in there. Besides, that James is a good guy. He wouldn't do something like this and you haven't pressed charges, so for all I know, it was the new guy that did this to you."

"Are you fucking serious right now? Are you really defending him and trying to accuse someone you've never met? Even though everyone at the church saw him hit me?"

"Looked like you were asking for it, bringing that new guy in."

Something pops inside me and I know if I stay here, I am going to burn this place to the ground. I feel the tears running down my face, boiling away from my skin instead of dripping off my jaw. "Fuck you and your bullshit. I quit."

He is shouting down the hall about how I'll never find another place to work that will be as good to me as I walk very carefully to the front desk and grab my things. I can't hold them in my hands, I'll melt it all. Hanging the purse over my arm, I head for the door. He shouts that he wants his keys. Standing with my hand on the cool metal of the door handle, I shout back, "You'll get them when I get my last paycheck!" Pushing through the door, I see the metal was getting soft and I've left a few ridges in it. Fuck. I'll just have to cool myself down on the drive. And touch the steering wheel as little as possible with my hands until they cool off.

Chapter Eleven

Matthew

When those two women from the church pulled up, I knew they would be trouble. My smoke form served me well as I followed them inside. I wish I was able to drink the blood of just anyone that pisses me off. Her boss would have been my lunch. Maybe I should tell the local shifter pack… since I know one of them now, that will have a vested interest in how Rick treated his little sister. Blaze seems to be having problems getting in her car. She is treating the handle like it is boiling hot. And now the steering wheel. What is up with that? Why is she driving with her wrists? Her face is awfully red. As I follow her back to the hotel, I make phone calls. The first one, to Frankie. Telling her that Blaze had a really shit day and I am buying a few bottles of wine for her. She is in her car and on the way before I can tell her where she needs to go. Once I have her headed in the right direction, I hang up with her. As Blaze turns into the hotel lot, I keep going to the store down the road. Tapping the screen of my phone, I call Chad next. "Hello?"

"Hi, Chad, this is Matthew."

"Oh! Hi! Are the results in?"

"They are. I can tell you what they are now or you can meet me at my hotel, where I have Blaze staying and I can tell you both together. Before you answer, you should know that she has had a terrible day today, and I think seeing you would brighten it a lot."

"The answer was yes, but now it is doubly so. What's the address?" I tell him and he says, "Perfect, I am about twenty minutes away. I'll tell the bar something came up and I need to go."

"I'll meet you out front. You can help me carry the wine up. I don't know what she likes, so I am getting a variety for her."

He laughs. "I'll see you there."

* * *

* * *

It takes me very little time to get the wine put into a couple of boxes and into my car. Pulling into the lot at the hotel, I see Chad standing out front. He spots me and I can feel him watching me park. By the time I am out of the car and at the passenger side, pulling out the first box, he is walking up. Straightening, I hand the first one to him.

As I reach into the car for the other box, he asks, "What happened that her day was so bad?"

I fill him in on the way inside, making sure to leave out bits that I can't know without her having told me. He looks like he knows that I am holding back, but I need my suspicions verified first. The guards I stationed in the hall look a little dazed. "Frankie is in there with her?"

They nod yes and I struggle not to laugh. She can be a whirlwind of energy when she feels the need. I knock on the door of Blaze's room and Chad asks, "Where do you stay?"

I point down the hall at the only other door here that isn't an elevator or stairwell. He nods as the door opens to reveal Frankie. She looks fierce until she sees us. She hugs me and, after releasing me, says, "Who's the guy with the box?"

He answers, "We're waiting to find out when we get in to see Blaze. You are holding things up. Going to let us in or continue your impersonation of a roadblock?"

She narrows her eyes at him. "Your friend does a poor impersonation of a comedian, Matthew. Hope that isn't his day job."

Chad laughs as she turns away from us and leads the way to where Blaze is sitting near the window. We set the boxes down on a side table and go to her. "So, I called Chad to come over because the results are in. Would you like to open them?"

Her mouth drops open. "Yes, I would. But what if the answer is no? I don't think I can take another bad thing today. Not without…"

"Without what?"

"Nothing. Let me have the results." That odd turn of phrase makes me wonder what she is hiding. I don't suppose I can be overly critical if she is hiding things from me. I have my own secrets to tell her, eventually. Handing over the envelope, I watch her face closely as she opens it. I think it will be a yes, based on the scent of the two of them and how they both seem to relax more when they are near each other, like they feel safe around each other. The smile playing at the corners of her mouth tells me all I need to know. It becomes a full smile as she looks up at him and says, "Hello brother! The results are positive! We are family!" She stands slowly, and he reaches out to help her. I step back to be out of the way as they hug. They read the results, and she tips her head to one side. "Wait, this doesn't say half brother and sister. This says we are full brother and sister. How is that possible?"

Chad shrugs, "We could ask our parents? I know my dad will answer if I ask, but he doesn't volunteer information."

"I can pretty well guarantee that my mother won't be answering any questions that might reflect poorly on her husband. Image is very important to her. Plus, we aren't really talking so much right now. They are still more than a little mad at me for not marrying their friend's son."

"What? Ok, we'll talk to my dad, our dad. If you want to meet him, that is? I can ask him alone if you don't want to meet him."

"No, I very much want to meet him. But, my face. I don't know if I want his first time laying eyes on me to be while I am bruised and battered."

I watch Chad put his hands on her shoulders and she looks up at him. "He is not going to think any less of you for the way you look right now. And, if I know my—our father, he has already seen you."

"You think so?"

"I do. There is no way she got pregnant with a second child by him accidentally. And that means that he has known about you and stayed away for a reason."

"If I had to guess, I would say my d—erm, her husband. My mom is still married to the man I thought was my father. Holy shit, she cheated on him! I was born like three years after they were married. What if he knew she, um, visited your father? Oh, my god." I need to sit down. Holy shit. My dad is not my dad and my mom cheated on my not dad and my father was out there somewhere probably spying on me?

Holy shit. "Didn't you say you brought wine? I think I would like a glass."

Frankie stands up from the chair near Blaze's. "That, gentlemen, is your cue to leave. We are going to sit here and drink up some wine and have a girls' night. Come back tomorrow with food and coffee." She pushes us toward the door and Chad walks around her to give Blaze a gentle hug as he tells her he will be back tomorrow and he'll bring their father to meet her whenever she's ready.

* * *

Blaze

Frankie gets Chad and Matthew out the door before coming back to sit in her chair, handing me a glass of wine as she does. "What a day."

I can't help but chuckle and then groan at the pain in my ribs. "Yes, that about sums it up. I just knew the day was going to shit when I saw Susan and Ethel get out of the car. Finding out Chad really is my brother is kind of the bright spot today, as long as I don't think too much about how that happened. Or that I have a father out there that I've never met but who has likely seen me. I don't know how to feel about that."

"I can imagine. Parents can be intense and not always terribly accepting."

"Yes. And mine are… more the not accepting of anything outside of their norms." Memories of fires flash in my mind. Fear and grandmother's house, learning to block it all away. Which isn't working so great these days. At least having Chad around calms it down. God, I could have had him around all this time if they hadn't kept us apart.

"Your parents don't accept you?"

"Not since I refused to marry the guy they had set up for me. Well, they weren't thrilled with my career choice either."

"Why?"

"They said Mowlen women shouldn't work, and especially they should not work in a field so grim and dirty."

"Well, that's some garbage. Mine aren't good either. It seems like a lot of people our age have less than great relationships with our parents."

"Exactly, and that is why quitting my job today is so fucking scary. I am my person, the only one that is going to catch me if I fall. It's also why I am so scared about relying on Matthew like this. I don't understand why he is helping me and what if he is really a monster in disguise? Maybe I jumped out of the pan and into the fire."

Frankie sighs. "Listen, I don't usually share this with people because I don't like talking about it. I'll share it with you so you can feel safer since I was in a similar situation when I met Matthew."

"What? Was he crushing on you, too?"

She laughs, "Ha, no. Ew. Not that he isn't pretty, just that he and I never felt that way about each other. Actually, I've never seen him really interested in another woman until you. You are the first one he has ever brought by the diner, too."

"Oh."

"So, I started working there years ago, when I was pregnant with my boy. He spends most of his time with his father these days, but you'll meet him eventually. I was working there and couch crashing, completely homeless and running out of couches to crash on because my parents would find out where I was staying and go harass the people I was staying with. My dad was super mad about me being pregnant so young. He actually tried to kill me when I refused to abort the baby."

"Wait, what? Are you kidding? Tell me you are kidding."

"Uh, sorry, can't. He really did. It was wild. But, I managed to not die. So, one day, Matthew comes strolling into the diner and ends up at one of my tables. He is a really friendly and kind man. So he was asking questions about the baby, you know, the usual stuff. I guess he could hear the tension in my voice because he asked more questions and somehow, it just didn't feel intrusive as it kind of was. I still don't understand that. By the time he had the entire story out of me, he was so mad. He was practically vibrating with it. He told me to stay there and not leave until he got back. Against all my better judgment, I did. "

"That must have been terrifying. You are really brave."

"Maybe. He came back and waited till my shift ended and asked me to go with him. I did because at that point I felt inside like it would be a good thing. So we leave and he drives me to this house. I was feeling some major anxiety. But I followed him in and after he led me in and showed me the stocked kitchen, he pulled out the keys he used to open the place and handed them to me. Said it was mine, and he wasn't taking no for an answer. I cried. And then I tried to make him take it back because why would a stranger do this? He refused. I did finally talk him into at least letting me pay him. Then he left me in this house. It took me a little while to get everything transferred to my name but, I did that for me. He would have left it that way. And, in all these years, he has never once been inappropriate. Or asked for anything in return."

"Holy shit."

"Yeah. Coming from my family and then losing my friends one at a time, this strange guy swooping in and literally saving me was terrifying. For about a year, I kept worrying that he was going to turn into some sort of psycho, try to force me into something, or who knows. Now, my boy is nearly grown, and he has been nothing but kind and a good friend. I almost feel bad for doubting him. If the world wasn't the way it is, I would."

"I can't blame you. But, gosh, I really appreciate you sharing your story with me. I feel a lot better knowing that."

"I remember how it felt to be scared and kind of alone. This time, it is within my power to help. How do you feel about new hair colors?"

"I feel like it's about time. I've never colored my hair. Let's go wild with it."

Chapter Twelve

BLAZE

What is that noise? It sounds like something hitting the wall over and over, ah, there. It stopped. Thank god. Dammit, there it is again. Forcing my eyes open, I look around the room, trying not to move my pounding head. The ceiling is still there, so that's good. Looking to the right, I see Frankie still sleeping in the bed next to me. The night rushes back at me, hair color and so much wine. Lifting my arm takes so much energy. That damned sound again as I pick up a chunk of my hair. I don't think that shade of red exists in nature, but I think I've seen something close somewhere. The banging noise starts again and I hear Matthew call my name. Fuck. He must be at the door. Rolling to my side, I push myself up, letting my legs swing toward the floor. The dizziness turns my stomach and I close my eyes, hand pressed to my lips to ward off the possibility of puking. Once it passes, I start easing my way to standing and then toward the door. Why is this room so damn big? At the door I hear Matthew say, "Let me in, Blaze. I've got coffee."

Opening the door, I tell him, "I was working on it. How did you know I was standing right here, anyway?"

"Because I could hear it when you hit the wall. Here's your coffee. Do you need help to the chair?"

"No. Just let me lean against the wall and drink my coffee for a minute."

"That color looks good on you. I brought food. It may sound odd, but I thought maybe you could try hummus and pita bread. Protein and carbs, it could settle your stomach." I watch from my spot against the wall as he takes things out of the bag he brought in. The pita smells warm and my stomach perks up at the scent. The hummus smells garlicky and I'm not really sure about that part, but the hunger increases as the coffee does its work. Pushing off the wall, I find I can walk a little more steady than when I made my way over here. He pulls out a chair for me and I sit, sucking down a little more coffee. The reality that I have no job hits me again, and I can feel the flames inside spiraling. Clamping down on them, I try to distract myself with the food. It tastes really good and my body kind of breathes a sigh of relief that I am eating. It gets a little bit easier to hold the fire in check. Frankie drops herself into a chair at the table and grabs the coffee. Raising my eyes from the food, I notice Matthew is sitting across from me.

"How long have you been sitting there?"

"Since right after you sat down." He chuckles. "You looked pretty deep in thought. I didn't want to interrupt you."

Groaning around another bite of pita covered in hummus, I shrug at him. "It might have been better that way. All I was thinking about was my lack of a job, how abysmal my savings are, and trying really hard to not panic. I've been looking for a new place to work for months and nothing. Now that Rick is telling everyone how terrible I am, my chance of getting a job are even less. I don't know what I'm going to do."

Frankie scoffs. "Fuck that guy. No one with any sense is going to listen to a guy like that."

"Well, they might think about it more right now while I am looking all bruised and battered. And it isn't like I can just lay around and wait until my face is all better. For one thing, I would go insane."

Matthew shakes his head. "I know a lot of people. One of my friends runs a funeral home. I could put in a good word for you. The owner was planning on expanding, something about a rivalry with one of the other places. Maybe take a couple days and go meet your father? Doing that will give you a little time to heal up more, at least the bruises. I know the ribs take longer. But, I don't mean to push. If you don't want to meet him, just forget I said that."

My mind is spinning. Hope and fear warring for top place as the flames inside rage. It feels like they will char me to ash. Something inside pops and I feel strange. Light-headed and foggy, but the fire is a little calmer. Almost like it is shocked. "You know, maybe I should take a chance and meet him. What is the name of the funeral home? I'll see if they have any applications I can submit."

"Don't worry about that. I'll have them call you, if you don't mind me passing them your number?"

"Sure, go ahead. And I'll send Chad a message. See when we can arrange to meet my father."

* * *

Chad replied back immediately and now I am out front, waiting for him to arrive. The whole family was there when he got my message and apparently our father howled with joy, causing everyone to get really interested in what was happening. So now I get to meeting them all today. Not exactly what I was thinking would happen. Holy shit. What if they hate me? What if I show up and most of them are mean to me? Maybe I should just go back inside and take a nap. Oh no, what if they think I am an idiot with all these bruises? As I turn around to go back inside and hide in my room, I hear Chad call my name. Shit. Turning around, I see him striding across the parking lot. He draws near and gives me a big hug that I happily return. "Where's Matthew?"

"He said he had some business to attend to, and he knew I would be safe with you all."

"He's not wrong. No one is beating you around our family. Come on, let's go before you chicken out."

"How did you know?"

"I could smell the feathers."

"You could not. I'm sure it was obvious, though. What are they like?"

"They are good people and they love you already. Our aunts are better than the FBI, and they know everything about you at this point. I am sorry to inform you, you will never escape their care and concern. They will be mothering you to death for the rest of your life. Sorry."

I can't help but laugh at the idea. "What about our father? What is his name?"

He waits to answer while we get in the car. As he pulls out of the space, he says, "Erik. Erik Vargr."

"What is he like?"

"He's quiet. Sad. But he's a good person. He's there when I need him, doesn't matter when or what. He's always been really tight-lipped about who my mother was and what happened to her. I can only guess that is because he didn't want to accidentally mess up her happy life."

"Happy? My-our mother isn't happy. She's almost never been happy. Her need to maintain appearances and... other things, have prevented that entirely. I am fairly certain she never wanted to marry her husband. At least, judging by the way she said some things. That's why I refused to marry the man they had set up for me."

"Wait, they tried to push you into an arranged marriage? Really?"

"Yeah. It's why we don't talk so much anymore. They wanted me to marry some guy right when I turned eighteen. I stalled, convinced them to let me go to college. Told them it was so I could have smarter babies. They had him at my graduation, with a ring. I ran away. Went home before they stopped looking for me and got my things. Left and never looked back. I've talked to mom some, but we just go round in circles about what she thinks I should do. He hasn't talked to me or acknowledged my existence since I left that day."

He steers the car into a driveway and stops in front of a little house that looks cozy. A man walks out. He is big. Blond like Chad and me. I think he might be even a little bigger than Chad. His hair is longer though, and I see the sadness in him. It's almost like a cloak swirling around him as he moves. He stops at the bottom of the stairs, crossing his arms over his chest as he plants his feet to wait. "That's him, isn't it?"

Getting out of the car, I feel almost in a trance. The flames in me have never been so quiet, so calm as they are right now. Something, something other is stretching. Flexing. I don't know what it is, but I know it is connected to this side of my family. Just as I know, the man I am standing before is my father, and now I wonder how I ever thought my mother's husband could have been my father.

"Welcome home, Blaze."

That sentence opened the floodgates, and I leapt at him, arms open. He caught me in a bear hug, my weight seeming to be nothing to him. "I have waited so long to meet you. So many times I saw you and couldn't speak, couldn't let you know. I'm so sorry I ever made that promise. I hope you can forgive me one day."

"There is nothing to forgive, I understand. I don't like it, but I think I understand. Would you tell me what happened? How all this came about?"

He squeezes me one more time and releases me as he steps back. "Do you really need to know? Sometimes it's better to let ghosts of the past sleep."

"And sometimes the daughter of your ghosts turns up and needs to know. Please tell me."

He sighs and seems to fold in on himself a little. "Very well. Come in. We'll sit in the kitchen and discuss old secrets before my sisters arrive."

* * *

I am sitting with my father in stunned silence when his sisters arrive. What my grandparents did, and the life my mother was forced into, I'm glad I had the strength to run away from it. And that thought is the last one I have time for as two women surround me with hugs.

"We thought we would never be allowed to meet you! That brother of ours holds his secrets so close, we despaired of ever getting it out of him."

"Yes! Tell us all about you! What do you do? What does your fur look like? Is it white like his?"

"Fur?"

Erik shouts at them, "What are you doing? She doesn't know about any of that! Fucking hell, did you even use your nose at all when you got here? She isn't ready to know that yet and now you've taken the choice from her!"

The blond in the white dress releases me and turns to face Erik while the one in blue tugs me off to one side of the table, whispering, "They get wild when they fight. It's best not to get in their way."

The one in white says, "The only reason she doesn't know, hasn't embraced what she was born with, is your refusal to let us find her. She has missed out on a whole world of experience because you made some stupid-assed promise to her mother! We've missed out on knowing her! All so you could honor a woman without the courage to stay! You be mad if you want, little brother, but she is going to know who she is today. If you had used your senses, you would have noticed the unfolding happening right in front of you. She'll change in the next few days, and there is nothing any of us can do to stop it. What were you going to do? Let her go home and terrify herself when it happened, and she didn't understand? Fuck you, Erik. You kept your promise, but I made no promises and I will do right by her if I have to take you on to do it."

His eyes flew to me as she told him off. I watch as they widen and then close, his face scrunching up like he is in pain. "You're right, Ell, she has to know now. I should have paid more attention. Thank you for always looking out for us all. Even if you are incredibly pushy about it."

Ell smiles at him before facing me, "You. Come back to the table. We need to talk about who you are."

The woman in blue whispers, "It will be ok. She's brash, but she always has the good of the pack in mind, and she will never steer you wrong. I'm your aunt Leann, by the way. Come on, I'll stick by your side."

I am weirdly comforted by this woman I don't know at all, saying she is going to stick by my side as we return to the worn table and chairs. There are only four chairs, but Chad never sat down. He has been watching from the door this whole time. He gives me an encouraging nod when I catch his eye. Leann nudges me into a chair, soft and sweet but as inevitable as the tides.

Ell sits across from me. "I know you've been kept in the dark all this time. There is nothing for that. Tell me, what do you know about your family?"

"Um, I'm not sure what you mean?"

"They've left you in the dark about everything except how to fight against yourself, haven't they?" She looks at my father. "You left her to these people. People that would hinder her growth just to maintain some stupid social standing with the humans? You have much to answer for, to her. You owe her for this."

My father hangs his head and I just feel so bad for him. She is berating him so much. "How is any of this his fault? He had no way of knowing what my life would be like. I feel like you are being unnecessarily harsh toward him and you don't know much more about me than he does. You've known me for less time than he has."

She smiles at me, and for some strange reason, I can almost see a wolf grinning at me. I blink and rub my eyes. The image is gone. "Little girl, I see the banked fire in you. I see the signs of a struggle with that fire, the char in your soul. I see the wolf finally freed from the box they locked it in, shaky and still weak, but stretching. Unfurling and growing into you. Now, would you like to know about the wolf side of your family, or deny your nature until you hurt someone?"

The horror and shame flood my being. Who else can see? What does she mean, wolf side? Oh my god, do I have something inside me besides the fire that could hurt people? "I don't want to, but I think maybe I need to."

"Good girl. We do what we must and we don't shy away

from the big scary things." She seems to approve of my decision as she looks at my dad. "Make some tea. One of the calming blends would be best." She turns to me and reaches out to take my hand. "I know you have a fire inside you, and your other family taught you to keep it locked away. While I don't know how to work with that power and cannot advise you on it and I am sorry for that; your grandmother did something much worse to you. She locked away the wolf side of you that is your birthright from this side of your family. Your fire has only recently burnt away what she did. If I had to guess, within the past few days. This is good. Your wolf is free. But you and your wolf have no training. No experience in managing those instincts. You are barely holding onto the fire. I can see the strain of it in you. I worry that without some training, you and your wolf will be out of control, in fear, and possibly hurting someone."

"I don't want to hurt anyone. How, what do I need to do?"

"You will need to come stay with us for a few days. We have rites and blessings that you should have had, ceremonies that will unite you with the wolf. Bring you into a unity that was always meant to be. That unity is what keeps you in balance, keeps you both safe. It's why you never hear of werewolves anymore. We learned how to unify and in doing, we gained so much. Our wolves became more than mindless beasts stuck in a human form for all but three days a month, and we were gifted in return with the use of their senses. I will teach you all of this. Everything, from the curse that first created our people to how we evolved. But, you must come stay with Leann and me until your first change is past. It will be soon. The moon is nearing full and your wolf will want her first run."

"I need to go get some things and tell Matthew something, but I will come stay with you. I've fought with my fire all my life and ever since I met Chad, it has calmed when he is near. Maybe if the wolf and I are working together, maybe we can find a way to work with the fire, too."

"That would be ideal, and I hope to see it happen. You are the first of mixed blood to have survived into adulthood. Most are murdered by one of the families. Mixing the two bloodlines has been heavily discouraged because it was magic that cursed us. We hold grudges really well. It is part of our nature as wolves. We remember what is not safe and have a natural aversion to it. Go, go get your things and Chad will bring you to my house. You will have a very long time to get to know your father. A few more days won't hurt."

* * *

Telling my father goodbye when I've only just met him was oddly emotional. I didn't want to leave, but under the watchful eye of Ell, I did. Chad waited till we got to the main road to say, "Well, surprise."

"Surprise, indeed. Knowing this makes me wonder, did you know I was related to you already? I mean, before the test?"

He grimaces and shrugs. "I was pretty certain you were related somehow. I wanted to say something, but you smelled off. So, I guess if your wolf was locked in a box, that would explain it. The fire was unexpected, though. You really have a fire inside you?"

"I do." As I watch the cars racing past us as he steers us toward Matthew's hotel. I hope he doesn't think less of me about this. "I have fought to control it since I was a little girl."

"How did you find out you had them?"

Please God, don't let him hate me when he finds out. "I was playing in a playpen with some other children. My mother was drinking with their mothers. I don't know why or exactly how it happened. My mother said that the playpen was suddenly on fire. All of us were burned at least a little. After that, she stopped the playdates. When I was nine, I woke up to my bed being on fire. I remember my, um, my mother's husband running for the fire extinguisher and putting out the fire. After that, he turned to my mother and told her to fix it. Fix whatever is wrong with her kid now or he would ship me off to boarding school until I was grown."

"Her kid? I thought you didn't know you weren't his until recently?"

He pulls into a parking space at the hotel and I look up at the windows of the building. I wonder if Matthew is home now? Is he waiting for me? What am I going to tell him? "I didn't. But if I wasn't behaving the way he wanted me to, then I was her kid. When I was behaving as expected, I was their kid. As important as image is to my mother, it is even more important to my father. Any whiff of something odd and he was all for shipping me off to some prison-like boarding school that would 'sort me out', as he put it."

I can hear him mumbling something as we get out of his car. Walking up to the hotel, he throws an arm around my shoulders. "You don't ever have to worry about getting sent away from our family. We know weird and nobody gets sent away for being different. Family is family, and we take care of our own, along with a few strays we've picked up along the way. I want you to know we aren't sending you away or abandoning you if you set the house on fire. We will insist you help rebuild it, but other than that, shit happens. Now, let's get your things. Have you decided what you want to tell Matthew?"

We walk through the doors into the hotel and I wait till we get in the elevator to answer. "I don't know yet. I can't really tell him the truth, now can I?"

Chad runs a hand across the back of his neck. "I think you might find him a lot more understanding than you would expect."

The elevator doors open to my floor then, and Matthew just raising his hand to knock on my door. He smiles as he turns to the sound of the elevator doors opening. My heart flutters at seeing that smile, knowing it's meant for me. Then reality sets in and it crumbles into dust as I realize this gorgeous man is not going to want anything to do with me if he finds out what a monster I really am. He meets me halfway, giving me a hug. "How was meeting your father? Do you have a new perfume on? You smell different."

"No, it's probably my aunt's perfume. Actually, my aunt asked me to stay with her for a few days so the whole family can meet me. I'll probably come back smelling just like her." Oh god, can he smell that I changed? How is that even fucking possible?

"Oh? Well, I'm glad you are getting to know your family. I talked to my friend at the funeral home today. They want you to come in Monday. I can tell them a different day if you need more time?"

Monday, fuck, what is today? Wednesday! "No, Monday is fine. I'll be back here Sunday night at the latest."

Swiping the card, I let us all into my room. I have to say I'm glad that housekeeping got rid of all the wine bottles. How even did we drink so much? I need to send Frankie a message and let her know I am out for a few days. I don't want her to worry. Hitting send on the message, I realize it is really quiet, for there being three people in here. Looking back, I see Matthew and Chad still in the entry, having what really looks like a whispered argument. That's weird. "What are you two whispering about?"

The two of them jump, turning guilty faces to look at me. Matthew says, "We are just talking about the best ways of keeping you safe from James. That's all, right Chad?"

Chad rolls his eyes. "Something like that. I still think you are being dumb."

Matthew glares at him and through gritted teeth, says, "You can think as you please, so long as you mind your business and not mine."

Putting my hands on my hips, I narrow my eyes at them. "That doesn't sound like protection talk. Is there something you need to tell me, Matthew?"

"Not unless there is something you need to tell me."

Ah fuck, well, he's got me in a neat little corner. "Nope. Actually, you know what? Shut the door. If you are going to hate me, then let's get this done now. I don't want to make this harder on us both just because I wasn't brave enough to tell the truth."

Chad's mouth forms an O before he grins and gives me a thumbs up as Matthew closes the door. "Ok. What did you need to tell me? I promise I won't be hating you for any reason, Blaze."

My nerves ramp up to warp speed and, with my hands clasped in front of me, I tell him. "I have been hiding that I am loaded the fuck down with fire since before I met you. It acts up at the most inconvenient times and I have to always be on guard to keep it from burning everything to ash. Then I met my father and his sisters today. A fire hazard isn't all I am. I am going to my aunt's house because apparently I am also wolf and neither of my families does anything by halves. So now that my wolf is free, I have to go learn how to be unified with it so I don't accidentally kill anyone. I think that's pretty much it. So, where are we going from here?"

Matthew walks over to the table, pulls out a chair, and seats himself. "I have to confess. I didn't expect you to tell me. So I wasn't prepared for this. Have a, have a seat." He waits while Chad and I both seat ourselves. "I have been keeping things from you, too. I don't know if today is the day for all of it. But, I'll tell you most of it and I promise I will tell you the rest after you have had time to process everything you have going on right now. Is that acceptable?"

I think about it for a minute. Do I want to know everything today? I'm honestly not sure I want to know a part of it tonight. Recent events, in addition to today, have been a lot. I can feel the tightness in my shoulders. "Can you promise it is nothing that will change things dramatically?"

"Yes, I believe I can promise that."

"Accepted."

"Ok. I am a type of vampire. Not the usual kind. I got mine making a deal with the gods. And that means the only blood I want is that of the desecrated holy person. I actually came back here on assignment. Imagine my surprise when you attend the church of the preacher I was assigned this time."

"There's a lot to unpack there. You meet with gods? Like, in person?"

"Yes. Not super often, but yes. I just met with one the day I first saw you in the café."

"Which one?"

"Odin. He's kind of a jerk, but basically a good guy. I think he would actually agree with my assessment."

Chad snickers and when I look at him, he shrugs, saying, "That is pretty well how he is depicted in the stories too. His exploits aren't always what one would say is strictly good. He did a lot of shit that could have been done kinder. But, overall, he does care and tries to do right. Say, the wolf Fenrir, he still looking to bite Odin?"

Matthew smirks. "Yes. He isn't always a wolf. But he always wants to bite Odin."

"I think I would like to hear more, but for now, my aunt Ell is waiting for me to get back. And I feel this odd sort of itching. I think she would want me to get back now."

Chad's face is suddenly closed, and he says, "Yes, let's get you back there. We don't need to rush, but it is time to go."

Matthew eyes us both and I know he has come to the same conclusion I have. The dangerous parts of me will be out to play soon and I need to get back now. "I'd like to come, if that is possible?"

Chad says, "You can, but you'll be waiting out front with me. She won't allow us in there."

While they talk, I grab my bag and stuff a few changes of clothes in, toiletries, and my laptop. Turning to them, I say, "I'm ready."

Chapter Thirteen

BLAZE

Chad is driving dangerously fast to get us to my aunt's house. The tires have squealed more than I want to think about and those lights were a lot more red than pink as he sailed through them. Matthew is right on his tail, so close I worry about what is going to happen when he stops. Another turn, my hands gripping the seat with everything I've got. Why is it so hot in here? My fire is quiet, calm even. Like a steady flame on a candle. Sweat is beading under my shirt, on my lip. My hands are slick with it. Chad slings the car into a gravel drive and slides to a stop in front of a house. The house looks old and big, but I've no time to stare as Chad is at my door, helping me out of the car and walking me into Aunt Ell's house. He opens the door without knocking and she turns in surprise. Her eyes land on me and she says, "Bring her this way."

We walk forever down a hall. So much wood here. This place scares me. What if the fire escapes here? This place would burn so fast. So many smells here. He guides me into a room where Aunt Ell is waiting. He leads me to a circle drawn on the floor. "Stand in here. It will be all right. I promise. Aunt Ell will help you through this. She guides us all through. Just trust her and work with her, ok?"

I nod, sweat dripping down my face at the motion. In the distance, I hear the door close. Ell's voice finds my ear through the haze. "Breathe with me. In one, two, three. Out one, two, three, four. She's there, inside. Look at her. She needs to be one with you. All you must do is accept her. Can you see her, Blaze?" Her voice weaves through my mind, calming me as I try to see inside. I find myself in the dark, a white wolf sitting across from me. She is emaciated, her fur dirty and unkempt. She is slumped forward a little, as though she is exhausted from a battle. I want nothing more in this moment than to comfort this sweet wolf. Extending my hand to her, I pause as she growls. "I won't hurt you. I didn't know what they had done. And I didn't know you existed until today. I promise, I just want to help."

Help? Will you become one with me? Join as we should have so long ago when the witch locked me in the box?

"The witch? My Grandmother did this to us? It was when I was sent there after my room caught fire, wasn't it?" The wolf nods, fumbling a little to stay upright.

If the fire hadn't set me free, I wouldn't be alive much longer. If we don't join, I probably won't be anyway, but at least I will die free of that hateful box.

"I will join with you. And next time Grandmother shows her face, perhaps we put her in the damn box." A fierce joy emanates from the wolf as she stands. I reach for her even as she leans in toward me. As we touch, the world turns into light and sounds and pain. I wake up some time later to find myself laying on the floor. A stretch and my hands are not hands. I can feel the wolf. She is with me, part of me, is me. I don't hear her speaking exactly, but I hear her in my mind.

You did it. We are one. We are healed.

Can you hear me when I think?

Of course. I could hear you if you spoke to, but it is much different in this form. We can't make the same sounds with our wolf's throat.

Are we going to be in this form forever?

No, we will move back and forth as we need or want. Ell is trying to get our attention.

I look up, and I see her standing there. Then she, she flows into her own wolf form. Walking over to me, she nudges me to stand with her nose. I am clumsy, with the two of us still learning to operate things together. We get to our feet and follow her as she leads us outside. I am unsure of how much time has passed, but it is night now. The moon is a silvery orb up high, glowing and gorgeous. A low, sweet howl slips from my throat before I really know what I am doing. It feels so right, though. Ell snorts and stomps her foot on the ground, turning her head to look at the woods. I know she wants us to run. One step forward from me and she takes off, running fast and free. Then I am running with her, the wind in my fur and a joy I have never known before in my heart. Even the fire is dancing inside us, but not trying to escape. It feels so content that I just let it be. And the three of us run with Ell till the sun lightens the horizon. She leads us back to her home, back through the same open door.

In the room we started in, she flows back into her human form. Kneeling in front of me, she says, "It is time to don your human form again. They have been waiting so anxiously to see you."

Just like that, I remember Chad and Matthew, both so visibly worried for me even as they tried not to show it. Even as I think we need to change, the world becomes lights and sounds again. I stumble and would have fallen if Ell hadn't been there to steady me.

She smiles so big, "You did really well, my little fire wolf. You integrated with her and it healed you both. Feel your ribs, your face. The bruises are gone. Come, let's feed you and let them see you before they pace holes in my floors."

Chapter Fourteen

MATTHEW

She has been in there for a day already. I can hear growls and whimpers of pain and it is driving me out of my damn mind with the need to go stop this, whatever it is that is hurting her. Chad assures me this is normal. Who fucking knows what normal is in this world we have entered into? A normal vampire bites who they please. A normal shifter has their animal as part of them from nearly birth. They don't spend so much time doing rituals to unite them while making their husband from another life tries to control himself out in the yard.

Chad eyes me again and pulls out his phone, tapping at the screen. Probably calling in reinforcements in case I go off the deep end. Turning away from him, I pull out my phone and call the funeral home. "Hello, let me speak to Quincy. This is Matthew."

"Quincy here. What can I do for you, Matthew?"

"I have decided we are going to expand. A lot. I want our funeral home to become the number one place for this area."

"That's great! I have so many ideas for how we could do this. But what brought this on?"

"The owner of the Sacred Home funeral home has offended me deeply. I want to put him out of business. And hire as many of his employees as will work for us. I don't want them to suffer any more than they have already at his hands. As of now, we pay the highest rates of any funeral home in the county. Everyone currently working for us gets a raise to accommodate their seniority as compared to the new hires."

Quincy is excited at the prospect of this big a project. He tells me of his plans and I think I should have spent more time listening to him during the times that I visited. After some time, he ends the call, saying that he must call an employee meeting now to tell everyone the good news. After the call is ended, I pull up the banking app on my phone and transfer a large sum to get him started. That done, an email to my accountant so they can monitor the account and the expenses, ensuring that they spare no expense.

When I turn around I find Chad did call in reinforcements, though not the kind I initially thought. Two of his cousins have arrived bearing bags of alcohol. "Matthew, I think you remember my cousins, Greg and Hollis. I know booze doesn't affect any of us for very long, but it is a way to pass the time while we wait. Care to have a drink?"

"I think I would like that very much. They aren't finished, are they?"

"No. And as night is falling, it's a fair bet they won't be finished tonight since they don't have the back door open."

"Why would that make a difference?"

"When it's done, they'll go run for the night, coming home only when the sun begins to rise."

"I see. I think we will need a lot more alcohol."

* * *

Blaze

The house smells faintly of alcohol and steak. Aunt Ell sighs, "The boys have been here keeping your brother and your lover occupied. There is nothing like steak after a long run. They'll have saved us some. Are you hungry?"

"Starving. How long have we been in here? It feels like weeks."

"It was three days and four nights. You were both so bound by that old witch that uniting you was… not easy. I would like to meet this woman. Perhaps speak to her at some length."

"Then you should meet her before I see her again. I promised to put the bitch in a box next time we see her. For what she did to us."

She stops me before we enter the kitchen. "You will need to learn your magic before you meet with her again. What she did was powerful, intricate magic. It was not done by someone who shuns their magic. She may not want you all to practice your magic, but I promise she has never stopped using hers."

That doesn't help the rage I feel about what she did to us. I tuck it away for later. The kitchen is full of people. As I enter, a cheer erupts. My family, how nice that is to think, my family is happy for me. They have surrounded me, hugging me and congratulating me. It is strange and a little uncomfortable. I've never had something like this happen before. Smiling and accepting it is painful in more ways than I care to look at. Someone presses a plate of steak and eggs into my hands and that is my escape. I tell them I am starving, which is no lie. They disperse at Aunt Ell's urging. I see Matthew leaning against a counter, his eyes never leaving me.

They are hypnotic. I feel I could fall into them forever, like maybe I did once. Someone bumps me and the moment is gone. Fading away like a dream with the light of day. Moving to stand next to him as I eat, I ask him, "Why do I feel like I've known you much longer than when I met you in the café?"

He moves to stand in front of me, trapping me between him and the counter, "They didn't cut your steak, you can't eat one handed without the steak being cut. Let me do that for you." His words are quiet and normal, but they are awakening something in me. Something that has slept a very long time. "That is what I held back from telling you. You knew me very well, once. A long, long time ago. Let me tell you a story while you eat?"

As if I could say no. I nod, and he finishes cutting the steak for me. Moving to stand next to me, I miss the heat from his body till he speaks. "A very long time ago, hundreds of years ago, during the time of the crusades, there was a happy couple. He was a duke, she a duchess. They were both very devout and, if the church willed it so, they did their best to make it happen. He was sent on a mission by the church, sent to fight people that had done no wrong. It was then that the man wrote his bishop and begged for lenience on these people. The bishop denied his request. When the man's neighbor requested to take possession of everything that belonged to the man as he had been gone a year on this mission and would obviously not be coming back, the bishop granted his request. Giving him ownership of the land, the castle, and the man's wife. She fought bravely, and was killed by the man. Left to rot in their marriage bed. When he arrived home, he fought his way through his own castle to find her desiccated corpse. The man tortured the truth out of the guards he had fought."

"Then he went to find the neighbor, and he killed him slowly. The bishop took longer took longer to get to, but he died in pain as well. When it was done and all was quiet, the man fell apart. There was nothing left to live for. Vengeance was done, and it did not bring her back. That was when the gods first appeared. The old gods and the Christian god. Imagine his surprise to find that the God he had been fighting for at the behest of the church was a woman. A goddess named Sophia. A goddess that abhorred what the church had become. They asked the man to fight on their behalf and they promised him the only thing that might convince him to make a deal with the gods, another chance to win her. Her choice, always her own. The promise was nothing more than that she would come back in another life and he would be allowed to try to win her love. Nothing more. No promises that she would be unable to resist him or any nonsense like that. No. Simply that he would be allowed to find her and attempt to win her love. And so the deal was struck. He would serve for the promise that one day she would return and maybe, just maybe she would love him once more."

I could almost see the story as he told it. The woman fighting to the death and her husband finding her. "Did he find her?"

"He did."

"Did she fall in love with him?"

"That remains to be seen. He is happy to have found her again."

Chapter Fifteen

Since my wolf and I were united in the ceremony, someone has come each evening to take me out for a night run. Matthew waits in the hotel lobby every night for my return. He hasn't pressed me at all since he told me the story. His presence is comforting, even though it causes a yearning in me for a deeper closeness. I don't know what I am going to do about it. My brother asks me when I will think about it, but the only answer I have for him is not right now. So much has happened. I feel like I need to process.

He doesn't seem to mind, so there's that. Today I am extra grateful for the uniting of my wolf and me because it healed us both. The bruises on my face are gone, as are the ones on my ribs. My wolf is healthy again, no longer looking like a half-starved and heavily abused creature. That lack of bruises is great for the interview today.

Matthew walks me to my car. It seems almost like what I read about courtships in the historical romance. He is just there, being steadfast and helping me. I want to dive in headfirst, but I'm so afraid that I'll be wrong about him. Or he may be wrong about me. What if I'm not the woman from the story? What if I fall entirely in love with him and she shows up out of the blue? Where does that leave me? No, for now it is safer for us to stay where we are, and I'll just keep pushing down on how much I want to kiss those lips of his. They look soft and strong, with that stubble to give the scratchiness. Ugh. Stop thinking about his damn lips!

"I'm sorry, I didn't quite catch that?"

"Oh fuck, was I saying that out loud? Forget I said anything, and you pretend you heard nothing."

One side of his mouth lifts in this sexy little smirk. "You could find out how the stubble feels."

Oh, my. We've arrived at my car and I turn to face him. He is so close. Oh. "I thought you didn't quite catch what I said?"

He steps forward and I'm pressed against my car, nothing more than a breath of space between us. "I didn't hear it all." He leans down, his lips next to my ear and my whole body trying to betray me and press against him. "The stubble part was what I actually heard. And the offer still stands. I could kiss my way along your beautiful neck, pressing the stubble into that sensitive skin. Or we could kiss and you would know how my lips feel on yours with the stubble on your face."

My heart is racing, and my wolf wants us to mate right now. Every inch of me wants nothing more than to press itself against him. "This isn't a good idea. In fact, I'm certain this is a terrible idea."

"Maybe today is a good day to be a little bad?"

And just like that, I've reached up and wrapped my arms around him. His lips meet mine and the world explodes into color. Our bodies are pressed against each other and it isn't close enough. His arms are wrapped around me, lifting me off the ground.

The cheers and whistles bring us both back to this world. We come up for air and realize a group of men has stopped to watch and cheer us on. He scowls at them and turns his back on them as he sets me down in front of him.

For my part, I am just trying to remember how to breathe right. All I really want to do is take him back upstairs and tend to this fire in my pants. I have to go to this interview. I can't blow it off.

Matthew clears his throat. "Perhaps I could take you out on a date, tonight if possible? If not, as soon as you are ready to let me take you on a date."

I try to speak and find that my voice isn't working quite right. Clearing my throat, I say, "Yes. Um, tonight would be good. Tonight would be really good. Interview. I need to go."

"Yes. Go to your interview. Good luck, and I'll see you later."

My hand reaches toward him, and he catches it in his own. Drawing it up to those lips, he presses a kiss to my knuckles. Oh, my. "Yes. Yes, I will see you tonight." He releases my hand and I get in the car. All my lips and a couple of other places throbbing with need. Focus, Blaze. You can do this.

* * *

Twenty minutes later

This place looks nice. I can't help but be impressed. And it looks like there are no less than three different contractors parked out front. Maybe they are expanding? When I walk in the front door, I see a woman at the reception area and head directly for her. "Hi, I'm here to see Quincy about a job?"

She smiles so big, it just makes me feel like I've come home. "Yes, darlin', I've been waiting for you to get here. Have you got a resume on you?"

"I do," I tell her as I pull it out of my bag. "Here's a current copy."

She takes it from me and flips back to the job history. I watch her skim it and find something that brings back that gorgeous smile that lights up her whole face. "You are definitely getting hired. Which means that we can be friends. My name is Falina." Her glorious, wild red hair flies back as she comes around the desk and takes my arm. "Come, I'll give you the tour. Currently, we have this area for viewings, it's lovely but we do only have the one right now. And if we go through here, we have prep rooms and a crematorium. All the usual things. Offices over here, garage that way. Bathrooms and break room down this hall. Gives us a little space from the dead people, you know? Ok, so let's go interrupt Quincy's meetings with the contractors. At this point, they are just bullshitting anyway. He'll be super excited when he sees your resume. "

"Why? It's not that impressive. Not that I don't want to be hired, but I am really curious why it would excite him."

"Oh, I should have mentioned that. Ok, so the guy that owns this place finally gave Quincy permission to do all the things he has been begging to do for a very long time. Technically, Quincy owns the place too, but the other guy is his mostly silent backer. Quincy's very own Sugar Daddy, so to speak. The guy that owns the Sacred Home apparently pissed him off. So he told Quincy to do what he wants, expand and put that guy out of business. But get this. He told Quincy that he didn't want any of the employees to suffer for it and to poach them if we can, hire them when they get let go if we can't. Even better, he wants us to have the most competitive wages too! We all got raises and you new ones are going to come in way above the average. Here we are," she raps once on the door and opens it. The four men inside turn to look at us and she just smiles. "Quincy, here's your first interview of the day."

He claps his hands together. "Fantastic!" Standing, he says, "Gentlemen, I think we are good. I am looking forward to getting those estimates and construction getting started." The men stand and say their goodbyes. Falina offers to show them to the front, since it is a bit of a maze. She gives me a thumbs up as she closes the door behind them.

Quincy gestures at the chairs in front of his desk as he sits down. "I noticed that Falina had what appeared to be a copy of your resume in her hands. Is there a chance you have another with you, or should I call her back in?"

"I have another copy." I grin as I hand it over. He unfolds it and does the exact same thing that Falina did.

I watch his face light up as he scans the work history. He looks at me. "The job is yours if you want it. I'm guessing that Falina filled you in on things after she looked at your resume?" After I nod, he goes on, "Good. I won't repeat everything. I do want to ask you a couple questions about your former employer, if you are willing to speak freely about your time there?"

"I am. He didn't exactly inspire deep loyalty."

"Excellent. What was the average pay rate there?"

"As low as he could bully a person into taking. He loved to talk about how expensive everything was and how he couldn't afford to pay people more and still keep his rates competitive for the clients."

"He what? I looked at what he is charging clients. His rates are the highest in the county."

"Yes. And everything he uses in a funeral is second rate

or worse. I could tell you stories about things he reuses. That's why I was looking for a job anywhere else."

"That's disturbing. How did he treat his employees?"

"That depended on standing in the church. Mine was not great and so he didn't treat me very well. Some of the older ladies he treated somewhat better. But not a whole lot. Can I ask you a question?"

"Of course! What's your question?"

"Your mostly silent partner. Would his name happen to be Matthew?"

"It would, Matthew de Montamore. Is that a problem?"

"No, not really. I just had an idea that it might be him. So, when do I start?"

"Officially, tomorrow. But we also have a ton of paperwork to get through, and you'll get paid for it as well. Falina will work with you on that. Can you find your way back to her, or do you need me to walk you out there?"

"No, I've got this. What time tomorrow?"

"Um, ten. Unless Falina wants you in earlier. And now, I have calls to return. Welcome aboard. See you tomorrow."

* * *

Blaze

Leaving the funeral home, I head directly to the diner. I don't even know if Frankie is working or not, but I need to talk to her. Pulling into the lot, I see her car parked off to one side. Thank fuck, because I just really need someone to talk to that isn't Matthew.

As soon as I walk in, she looks at me and nods at the far end of the counter. I sit down and she comes over pretty quick. "Are you ok? I haven't seen or heard from you in days!"

"Shit! I'm so sorry. I went to meet my father and the whole family wanted to meet me. It ended up a whole thing."

And then there is the wolf bit, but we aren't going to talk about that. "That went fine. But Matthew… we need to talk."

"Oh, girl. Give me ten and I'll go on my break."

It seems like hours go by before she comes to sit next to me, "All right, spill. I've only got half an hour."

I tell her everything about today. The kiss, the kiss that still gives me shivers. The job and the fact that he neglected to mention that he was part owner and is now waging a war against my former employer.

When I finish, she is laughing. "What are you laughing about? This is serious."

She pats my arm. "At some point, you are going to realize how hilarious this is. For now, you have a guy that does fun things to your lady parts without touching them and is waging a war against your former employer for you while getting you a job that allows you direct participation." She puts an arm around me and leans her head on mine. "Listen, this is just things starting to go right for you. I know it's scary as fuck. But it will be ok. For now, go with it. We know for sure that Matthew is no James, so that concern is over. What more do you really have to worry about?"

"What if he changes his mind one day and decides he doesn't want me? What if he breaks what is left of my heart?"

"Oh honey, what if he just walks with you while you heal?"

"Men do that?"

"Some do. Matthew is one of the few good ones. Just give it a chance. Either way, you'll have a good job out of it and that's something, right? And what if it works out all the way around?"

"Maybe you're right. Maybe I just need to put on my big girl panties and see where this goes."

"That's my girl! Now, what are you going to wear tonight?"

Chapter Sixteen

Matthew

Once Blaze left, I did too. The good pastor left for a three day retreat this morning, making today the perfect day to spend some time searching through his computer. The area is deserted when I drive through. Parking a fair way from it in a shaded spot and making sure there are no cameras or people about, I let myself become vapor and float out of the car through a barely cracked window. Inside his place, I reform once I get into the study. The computer is sitting there, still on. Touching the mouse brings up the login screen. Luckily, I've been watching him and I know the password.

A few keys tapped and I'm in. I start out by poking around in the files. A few look promising, so I plug in a drive and copy them to that. Once I've been through it all, including his porn stash, I turn to the browser. When I open it, I check the saved sites and find a popular cloud storage. Clicking that brings up files that are just terrifying.

This church he heads, of which this location is but one, is nearly ready to take over the country financially. If these documents are right, they have soldiers in many more key places than I am comfortable with. I copy things to my file and erase the record of what I have done. Putting the computer back to sleep, I race out of there and back to my car. I need to talk to the gods now.

I call for them all the back to the hotel, not a one of them answers me. I race up to my room at the hotel and Blaze is in the hall waiting. Fuuuuck. She doesn't look happy and I cannot brush her aside to go and fruitlessly call the gods when they aren't looking to answer me. I can put this drive away while she is with me.

"It appears you are not happy with something I have done. I very much want to hear it and correct it however I may. But I need to get this put away," I tell her as I show her the drive. "Are you willing to walk with me into my room and tell me as I put it away or wait in there while I do?"

She nods, still unhappy but willing to work with me. I pull out the card key for my door and let the two of us in. She is silent and moves to stand in the seating area while I head for the bedroom where I have a small safe in the floor under the bed. Not the easiest place to get to if you don't have supernatural strength, but that's why it is perfect for me.

When I come back out, she is still standing, staring out the window. She is breathtaking. The long blond hair, those curve, good gods, those curves. As if she can sense my eyes on her, she turns and catches me staring. The slightest lift of her lips tells me she isn't mad about that, so I decide to dive in.

"So, you seem displeased. Want to tell me about it?"

"I know who owns the funeral home I was hired at today. And who has started a war against my former employer. I talked to them and I know that you technically stayed within the bounds of what I asked." By the time she gets this far, I am holding my breath. Have I fucked up the little ground I gained? Then she goes on, "So I'm going to let it pass this time."

The relief that floods my body at those few words is immediate and intense. "Thank you, I appreciate your tolerance. I apologize for being deceptive. I promise, I will be fully transparent from now on, instead of withholding key details that might sway your decision. Are you still going to take the job?"

She smiles. "Yes, I love the place and the people. Falina especially. And, maybe I'll go to hell for it, but the idea of working in the place that is working to put Sacred Home out of business kind of makes me happy."

Crossing the room to stand closer to her, I tell her, "I can assure you that she would not be sending anyone to hell for a petty revenge against a shitty person."

"I forget you talk to God."

"Gods, and the one you are referring to is a woman. She is still quite pissed about the whole changing of her gender in all of her books."

"Oh, I would be too. Why doesn't she do anything about it? I mean, she's a god. Can't she just snap her fingers and do the thing?"

"I don't know. Every time I've asked about things like that, they've dodged the question and left soon after. Um, are we still on for dinner?"

She lifts one shoulder in a shrug and smiles. "Yeah, I think I would like to explore that a little more."

Frissons of excitement run through my body at her words. It's all I can do to keep my pants from becoming a tent. "I need to shower and change. If you are ready, you are welcome to stay here and wait. Or join me in the shower and we'll order in."

The blush of her cheeks is sexy as hell and for some weird reason, it makes me as hungry as one of those damned desecrated priests. "No, I need to shower and change as well. I'll meet you in the hall?"

"I'll see you there."

She practically runs out of my room and I head for the shower, thoughts of her running through my heads.

* * *

Blaze

After running out of his room and into mine, I realize I have no fucking clue what I am going to wear out on this date. Grabbing my suitcase, I toss it on the bed and paw through it all. I don't worry about this very often. Maybe I should? Ok, here's a pair of pants not made of denim. We can work with this. What do I put on top? Red silk shirt from the thrift store? Maybe. Black sweater with sparkle bits, no. Too hot. Black silky feel tank with a lace cardigan? Snatching my interview clothing off, I have a moment of panic about my panties. The ones I wore today are plain cotton thongs. Maybe I should hunt up a prettier pair? I don't have time for this. Fuck it, no panties, it is. It's one less layer to peel off for what I really hope happens tonight any way. As I pull the pants on, it occurs to me how horrified my mother would be about my hopes for tonight. Good girls wait till they are married. I can hear her voice in my head saying that tired line.

Pulling on the red silk with the fluttery sleeves and v-neck, I pad over to the bathroom mirror. Not bad, but I don't know if I am feeling the red tonight. Switching shirts, I wonder how many times did my grandmother drill that into my mom's head after she fell pregnant with Chad? How bad was it for her that she chose to give her son to his father's family? And what kind of weird connection do they have that she couldn't have a baby with my, no, with her husband? I wish I could just ask her. Back in front of the mirror with the black tank and lace cardigan, yes. This is the one. The spaghetti straps and slouchy neckline are draping great over my boobs. The cardigan gives me the feeling of having more coverage while still letting him see my shoulders, which are broad and strong and I feel like are pretty sexy. Turning and twisting, I get an idea of what the back looks like. If he likes big butts, he isn't going to be sad about mine. The pants are form fitting and the way the cardigan kind of rests on the top gives it a nice frame.

Makeup. Uh, fuck. Ok, my face is fairly good. So, eyeliner. Accent those eyes, add some mascara and darken the brows a little. Especially since I get white eyebrow hairs now, the fucking audacity. Some warm red lip gloss to keep my lips from turning into some sort of scaly desert and causing me to be wildly self conscious about them. Hair, uh, shit. Yeah. Run a brush through it and a little smoothing oil. It's going to have to be enough.

Heading for the door, I grab my purse and realize I don't have any shoes on. Fuck me. Black heels, of course, they are in the bottom of the suitcase. Fabulous. Once I get them in my hands, putting them on as I head for the door is a snap. Oddly enough, since I have been going on these runs, my balance is way better.

When I step out into the hall, he is there waiting. My breath catches for a moment. Those pants are doing nothing to hide his package. He may as well be wearing grey sweats. Sweet mother of god, I think he is half hard just looking at me. Or maybe it's because I am staring at his dick. His eyes are further up. Over that chest clad in a black button-up shirt that is definitely hugging his form. Those blue eyes are mesmerizing. If we don't have sex tonight, I may die. "Hi. What is that scent you are wearing? You smell delicious."

He smirks. "I'm not wearing any cologne. I am really pleased that you think I smell delicious."

"Oh. I am in so much trouble."

He crosses the hall to thread my arm through his and says, "Only if you don't want this as much as I do. In which case, we are both in trouble. Let's go to dinner now, before I start trying to talk you out of these clothes."

I didn't know elevator rides could take so long. I also didn't think about how not wearing a bra meant I was going to be head-lighting everyone. My nips could cut glass right now between how good he smells and the movement of the fabric over them. Oh, I did not think this through.

His car is parked in the drive in front of the hotel, a perk of being the owner, I guess. In the car he asks if there is a kind of food I don't like. "Um, food that isn't for me? I haven't found a type of cuisine that I don't enjoy. Well, no. I don't enjoy bugs as cuisine. I understand it is fine dining for some and necessary for others, but I just can't."

I can see him trying to hold back laughter. "I think we can accommodate a bug free dining experience. How do you feel about seafood tonight?"

"That sounds great. My family has pushed a lot of red meat on us lately. My wolf and I aren't really super fond of that much red meat. Chad says it's because of the nightly runs. They think I need more protein to muscle up my wolf. She doesn't agree, she says all she needed was me. And to be out of that damnable box my grandmother put her in."

"I can imagine that hurt both of you. Any idea why she did it?"

"Guesses based on what are probably half truths. For one, she is the only one in my family that knows how to use her magic, and according to her, it is a terrible sinful thing that we must never use. But I have vague memories of things floating across rooms when she thought I wasn't looking. And then there is the family reputation, that was always super important. She didn't want me to sully our reputation, whether it was by setting something on fire or, I suppose, by turning into a little wolf. I don't understand why appearance would be so important to her. I keep thinking about what my mom must have gone through, being raised by her. And then coming home pregnant with my brother. My grandmother must have lost her mind over that."

He guides the car into a parking space and turns to me after putting it in park. "No part of you is bad. Though you look damned sinful in that, and my thoughts are living in the gutter since I met you. I'd prefer it if you didn't set my things on fire, but if you want to walk around in wolf form, I could find a leash and collar for you."

He is snickering as he says the last part and I can't help but laugh at the picture. My wolf and I are in full agreement that no one is putting a leash and collar on us, for any reason. "Take me in and feed me before we decide to take a bite out of you."

He laughs as he gets out of the car. I turn to get out, but before my hand touches the handle, he is opening it for me. "Aren't you worried someone will see you?"

"No. People tend not to see me unless I am directly interacting with them."

"Really? I saw you the minute I entered the café."

"Oh? You hid it well. I didn't think you had even seen me."

"I did. I was busy telling myself that I was engaged, and I needed to ignore you. Then you caught my coffee cup, and that went out the window. So what is this place?"

His face says he is fully aware of why I changed the subject, but he goes along with it. "This is Puffers. It is a seafood restaurant. They don't actually serve pufferfish, but the name entertained the owners, so they kept it. They do serve a full seafood menu and the food here is phenomenal. The atmosphere is classy and still manages cozy. It's an interesting crossing and I hope you will enjoy it."

I look around at the place as we wait in the line to be seated. The place has really elegant lines, a muted gray for the walls with dark green accents. The lights are soft, casting a glow over each table without being too bright. It's the chairs that really catch my attention. The backs look like very well cushioned seashells in the same dark green as the accents. The people sitting in them look so comfortable for all that they are dressed fairly nice. We get to the podium and the guy there exclaims, "Matthew! Why didn't you get my attention when you came in? You know I wouldn't have made you wait."

He shrugs, "I know. I just don't want to make everyone else wait for me. Besides, it meant I got to watch Blaze take in your place for the first time."

The man notices me and looks back at Matthew. "You brought someone?" He looks back to me, "Blaze, I am so happy to meet you! My wife is going to be out here to meet you as soon as she finds out Matthew brought someone with him. I am so happy to meet you, I said that already didn't I? My name is Gary, my wife is Sharon. You'll see her soon enough. For now, let's get you seated." He leads us through the restaurant to a quiet little booth set behind a little wall of greenery. The window looks out over the city, a view I have only seen from my room at Matthew's hotel. I wait until Gary is gone to ask Matthew, "How did they get this view from a one story building?"

He chuckles, "Magic. That's why booths like this are really exclusive. Gary is a different sort of a creature all together, his wife is an outcast witch. Your family isn't the only one that has very strict rules about things, from what I understand. The type of creature that Gary is apparently offends the shit out of her family."

A woman's voice comes from the other side of the table, startling me. "It's ok. You can tell her what he is."

Matthew sighs. "Popping in like that isn't cool, Sharon."

She laughs loudly. "I'm fine with not being cool. We usually let people think my husband is some sort of creature, but in reality, he is a genie. The genie if you've read the fairy tales. My family looks down on them for being enslaved as their public stance. In reality, he scares the shit out of them with the amount of power he has. He could crush most of them in one fell swoop, and they don't like that idea."

"Really? Why? He seems so nice."

She smiles brightly at me. "Matthew, you picked a good one. Bring her back. He is so nice. He is the kindest, most understanding man I have ever met. Don't get me wrong, he is dangerous to those that would harm his loved ones. For a time when my family was harassing me, I was really afraid he would lose control and end them. That is mostly in the past now. I'll let you enjoy your dinner, Blaze, you come here any time. We'll take care of you. Anyone that Matthew would actually bring here is good people. Admittedly, the sum total is one, but that just makes you all the more special. Enjoy your dinner."

She is gone before I can get another word in. "Wow, she is something. I think I love her a little bit."

Matthew chuckles and drapes an arm across my shoulders. "Yeah. Her and Gary are great people. She meant what she said, too. If you ever find yourself in trouble and I can't get to you for some reason, come here. Nothing will harm you here. It doesn't matter the hour, whether they are open or closed. You just knock on the door if the place is closed. They'll appear."

"Holy shit. I really need to learn how to do cool things with my magic. Cooler than just setting things on fire, that is."

Plates of food appear on the table in front of us. I fucking love this place. Drinks and utensils wrapped in black napkins appear while I am still marveling at the food appearing. "We didn't even order. How did they know what to make for us?"

"I've never been able to figure it out and they aren't telling. They are always spot on, so give it a try."

The food is divine. We are both quiet as we enjoy the food fully. The drinks compliment the food, and I don't even really know for sure what any of it is. By the time we finish, Gary has come by to tell us that our meals are on the house and if we try to argue, he is sending Sharon. Matthew laughs and declines to argue. He waits till Gary leaves and pulls a bill out of his wallet, writing on it. This is a tip. I laugh as we leave the restaurant. Gary glares playfully at Matthew as we pass the podium.

Outside, Matthew asks if I would like to walk a little. "Yes, that sounds nice. Are we going to drive there?"

He pulls me into his arms and I wrap mine around him. He squeezes me close to his body as he says, "We aren't driving there."

I feel my feet lift away from the pavement and I am very glad he is holding me tightly as I squeeze my eyes shut. The sensation of moving through the air is strange and I open my eyes a little, peeking at the ground moving so fast under us. He brings us back to the ground, landing so gently I didn't realize at first that my toes were touching the ground. "Where are we?"

"A walking path that is technically closed at sunset but they aren't patrolling, so I think we are safe to wander the place."

Looking around, I see we are on a path. The greenery is abundant, and the air filled with the scents of jasmine and honeysuckle. The moonlight is shining down on us, bright and silver light bathing everything. "Matthew, it's beautiful."

"Not so beautiful as you."

My heart feels like it will burst with joy. I've never been so spoiled. Admittedly, he has a leg up on everyone being able to take me to these magical places. He takes my hand and we start walking down the path. I marvel at the beauty revealed in the night. "You know, I was always told that we shouldn't go out at night. It's too dangerous. I think maybe they didn't want me to see this beauty and live a life in the moonlight. Or maybe they were afraid of the fairy tales about werewolves."

He laughs, "Perhaps they were afraid you would find the vampire of your dreams while you were out wandering the night."

"Perhaps. You know, I had forgotten about the dreams."

"What dreams?"

"I dreamt about a man that loved me and was always searching for me, never finding me. He was so sad. I used to wake up crying and telling my mother that we had to find the sad man. She said it was just a dream and told me to go back to sleep. Eventually I stopped waking her up about it, stopped telling her anything."

"I'm sorry that she couldn't accept you or your dreams."

"It's not your fault. She just couldn't accept it because it wasn't part of the normal family we had to be. Knowing more about me is actually kind of helping me to not be so mad at her. I feel like she was in a really rough place and just doing the best she could with what she knew. I think I am ready to go back now."

He turns to face me and opens his arms. I step into his arms, wrapping mine around him as he holds me so close to him and we lift into the air.

Chapter Seventeen

Blaze

Back at the hotel, I'm suddenly nervous. I don't know what to do with my hands, with me. He walks me to my door, and I feel like I'm missing a chance. "I would invite you in for a drink, but I left my room a mess."

He brightens, "Would you like a drink? I have a small bar in my room."

I could cry with relief. "Yes, I would love a drink."

The few steps to his door feel filled with promise. He lets us in and I shrug off my lace cardigan, as if it would cool me off any. Following him to the bar, I watch as he makes two drinks. He slides one over to me, his fingers lingering on mine till he withdraws to pick up his own drink. I sip my drink and then he is next to me. I can feel the heat of him on my arm.

"I've never done this."

He sets his drink down and sits on one of the stools. "What do you mean, you've never done this?"

"I mean, the two people I've had sex with were people I had been in relationships with for months before we had sex."

He grasps my arm and tugs me to turn and face him. I take one more sip of my drink and, setting it down, I turn to him. He takes my hips in his hands and pulls me into the v of his legs. "I haven't been with anyone since my wife died."

My hands go to his shoulders, those broad shoulders that feel so nice under my hands. He hums a little at my touch. "Why not? I get the impression that you have been waiting a very long time for her to return. Why not take a lover while you wait?"

He shrugs, his muscles shifting under my hands. My hands start to explore his shoulders of their own volition, and I just let them. "Because there wasn't anyone that I was willing to let touch me." His voice is getting a little breathy and I enjoy seeing the effect I have on him just by touching his shoulders. Slowly, I explore his neck and then his scalp, watching his eyes roll back and close. "Oh gods, this feels so good. No one has touched me in so long."

"Not even a hairdresser? Barber?"

"No, my hair does as I need it to. I have no need for one."

"That's convenient. Are there any places you don't want touched?"

"By you? No."

I run my nails lightly down his scalp to his shoulders and he moans. Leaning forward, I run my hands down and up his back. His breath hisses through his teeth. Straightening, I move my hands to his chest, smoothing and exploring. "Mind if I unbutton your shirt and touch your skin?"

He makes a noise that sounds almost pained as his hands go to the middle of his shirt and with one swift tug, buttons go flying all over his very modern room with all its dark, mirror-glossy tiles.

My hands waste no time finding his skin. "What if I'm not her? What then?"

"I'm done looking, even if you aren't her. You are the only woman I've wanted in centuries. If you aren't her, then I don't want her. You are the one I can't get out of my mind. The one whose lingering scent in the hall fills me with longing." His eyes snap open and his arms crush me to him as he leans down and takes possession of my mouth. His tongue invades me, but I opened the gates. When he releases my lips, he whispers, "You are the one I want. This you, in the here and now. Only you. You are the one that I will worship tonight until you beg me to fill you."

Oh, sweet jeebus, yes. My voice is failing me, so I just nod. Something dark flashes in his eyes as he lifts me off my feet, his lips on mine. My feet touch the ground again and his hands are pushing the hem of my shirt up. I lift my arms into the air, watching his face as he reveals my bare skin. He looks hungry as he drops my shirt to the ground. His fingers make quick work of the fastening on my pants. That gorgeous mouth of his latches onto a nipple. Pleasure floods my body from the sensation of his tongue and teeth.

My pants are on the floor, and his hands are everywhere. His mouth leaves my breast, and a sob escapes me for the loss. Then he is on his knees in front of me, pushing me back. I realize the bed is behind me and I let myself fall back. His hands are spreading my knees as I land, he presses kisses up my thighs. Then his hands are on my hips and he drags me down the bed till I can feel his breath on my pussy. His tongue delves into my folds, making me cry out with pleasure I've never felt before. I finally know what all the women were talking about online when they said it was amazing, as his tongue does magical things that have me squirming and thrashing, moaning so loud but unable to keep quiet. He creates a suction on my clit and I think I might die. The pleasure becomes so intense and then I shatter, every thing that was me in floating in millions of pieces. He lifts his mouth from me, his eyes dark and intense. "If you want to stop, now is the time."

"I wouldn't stop now for anything. Fuck me, please, please, fuck me."

He looks up at the ceiling briefly. "How can I say no when you beg so pretty? Scoot up on the bed."

I do exactly as he told me, scrambling back to be fully on the bed. Watching him crawl up toward me, I get a deep desire and I flip over, putting my ass in the air. He groans, "Oh baby, there is nothing I like more than your ass in the air waiting for me."

I feel the bed dip as his knees settle between mine, his hands gripping my ass. One hand leaves my ass as I feel the head of his cock pressing into me. I press back just enough for the head to slide in. Oh fuck me, he feels so damn good. He pushes into me, excruciatingly slow. Then he is buried in me, my ass pressed against his pelvis as he holds still, panting. "Oh fuck, Blaze, be still. I'm going to cum before I mean to if you keep moving."

I can't help myself and I make circles with my hips, his fingers digging into my hips as he groans. Next thing I know, he has snatched my torso up off the bed. One hand at my throat and one on my clit. He growls in my ear, "If I'm coming now, you're coming with me."

He pounds into me with his cock, the hand on my clit rubbing it just right. "Oh god, oh fuck, Matthew!" He kisses my neck and I tip my head to one side to give him better access. Then he bites me and the world explodes with me. He thrusts into me one more time and cries out my name.

Suddenly, the bed feels really hot. I open my eyes and realize I set the bed on fire. Fuck! I wasn't paying attention, and it got out of control. "Matthew, shit, Matthew, the bed. It's on fire."

A muttered shit and suddenly I am across the room. He has a fire extinguisher and is putting out his bed. Once it is out, he looks over at me with a grin. "So, it was that good for you?"

The laughter bubbles up and we are both standing there, naked, sooty, and laughing. I think I've never had a better time in my entire life.

* * *

Matthew

I can't believe she is here. Or well, that I am here in her bed. I've waited so long for this moment and it is even better than I imagined it could be. She looks so peaceful sleeping. I know she has to get up soon, but I am loath to wake her. I know she is going to feel bad about setting the bed on fire, but I would sacrifice a thousand beds to have last night. Now, I'll just get sheets and mattresses that are more flame retardant and plenty of fire extinguishers in case the first plan fails.

I'm still watching her sleep in the morning light when I feel a presence in the room. Turning my head, I see Odin and Sophia standing in the room. Fucking hell, this is not when I wanted to see them. Sliding away from Blaze as gently as possible, I get to the edge of the bed and grab the shorts I wore over here last night. Slipping them on and standing in one smooth motion.

Odin raises a brow at me. "No morning wood sleeping next to a beauty like that? Sure you like women?"

"She set the bed on fire last night because she lost control from the pleasure and we moved over here to continue and eventually sleep. I like women just fine. I am currently quite satiated."

Odin laughs loudly, waking Blaze. She sits up with the sheet held to her, a panicked look on her face. "Who are you?"

Sophia glares at Odin before turning to Blaze. "Don't mind Odin, he lost his self control and consideration somewhere after they were cut off in a fight he started. I am Sophia. You know me as God. Please, do not call me God. I am still furious about the way they misgendered me."

"O-ok. I, um. Hmm. Do you all need to be alone to talk? Should I leave?"

"Don't be silly, you are welcome to be here. In fact, we'll turn away so you can dress. I know you'll feel more comfortable that way."

Odin puffs up. "I didn't say I would turn around. I bet those boobs are nice and I would like to see them!"

Sophia's countenance darkens and little bits of energy pop in the air around her. "You'll give her privacy while she dresses or I'll take your other eye. And then, I'm going home with you to explain to your beautiful wife why your eye is residing in a baggy in my pocket instead of in your big, thick skull. I can only imagine the fun that will be had after I leave."

I turn away to avoid Odin seeing my smile as he clears his throat. "You know, it would be ill done of me to intimidate a human into showing parts they clearly don't wish to share with me. I'm just going to turn away and let you have a bit to get dressed, Blaze. Give a shout when you are decent."

I can hear Blaze moving and putting her clothes on. We all turn when she says, "I'm decent now."

Odin looks disappointed, while Sophia seems quite cheerful. She looks over at me and asks, "What was it you wanted to talk about yesterday?"

I start the process of making coffee as I tell them about

what I found. Blaze comes over to lean against the counter and watches the coffee percolate as she listens. As I finish, I ask them, "Why didn't any of you answer yesterday?"

Sophia and Odin exchange grim glances before he says, "We were otherwise occupied. It is related to what you are seeing. This preacher has more power than even his church organization realizes. He needs to be taken out now. Unfortunately, he has grown too powerful. You are going to need to call in some of the others."

Blaze looks confused. "Others? How many did you recruit? Are you not the only one?"

"I am not. And some of them are fairly volatile toward certain deities."

I pour the coffee for Blaze and myself while Odin grumbles about Fenrir. Sliding Blaze's cup closer to her, I turn around with my cup in hand. "Why do I need help for him? None of us usually needs help of any sort. They are just human. I've only taken this long so I could gather information first."

Sophia is the one that breaks the silence. "He isn't completely human anymore."

"Define not completely human anymore, please."

"Gaining powers at a pace we are mightily uncomfortable with considering what he plans to do with those powers." Odin scowls at Sophia for answering and she tells him, "Keeping them in the dark doesn't help anyone. I think we should tell them more."

"We agreed we were going to keep things on a need to know basis with the humans."

Sophia throws her hands up. "They aren't human! She is a hybrid wolf and witch. By the by," she looks directly at Blaze, "your grandmother is still mad about that. And he is a vampire, not even the regular kind, but a special, altered kind that we created."

Clearing my throat, I wait till they are looking at me. "Speaking of me being a special breed, I have a new craving lately. I wondered if you could tell me why?"

Odin grins. "That was a little something that Freya and I cooked up. When you are mating with someone, they become someone you can feed from. You don't need much blood, anyway. Call it a perk."

Blaze is smirking into her coffee. "That explains something from last night."

"Sorry about that. I wasn't expecting that to happen. Since I knew I was having strange cravings. I should have controlled myself better."

She laughs. "Did I seem bothered by it? I'm good with you biting me. If anything, I need to work on not setting the bed on fire. Of the two, I think mine might be more destructive."

Sophia gets a strange look on her face. "You will find your teacher soon. She is waiting for you."

Blaze nods, biting her lip and becoming very interested in her coffee cup. "As for you, Matthew, call the others to you. They will be needed. We will be in touch soon."

* * *

Blaze

After the morning's events, a new job almost seems like a letdown in regards to excitement. Falina is really nice though and Quincy asked me to work with her this first week, till I know where everything is. We are working to clean and sanitize a room after a guest has been cleared when she asks how I feel about witchcraft. I sort of freeze and turn to look at her. The relief rushes through me when I realize she is nervous about my answer. "I don't know a whole lot, but I need to learn."

Her eyes light up. "It's fire, isn't it? I can smell it on you."

"What do you mean when you say you can smell it on me?"

Falina shrugs and carries on with mopping. "It isn't like smelling it with your nose. But smelling is the best way I can describe it. I can smell the fire dancing in you. And something else, that I'm not really sure what it is. I haven't smelled it before. Oh, and before you worry that you are spilling all your secrets to some weird normie, I'm a witch too. My gifts are more earthy though. I never had to worry about setting my room on fire or anything else. At least, not directly. I did have to worry about setting off tiny earthquakes. Those can inadvertently cause a fire. Or just bring your ceiling down on your head and that is no fun."

"I don't guess it would be. Unfortunately, my accidental fire starting days still aren't over. I accidentally set my bed on fire last night. At the worst possible time."

Falina stares at me, waiting for me to share. My cheeks heating with a blush, I tell her, "It was during an orgasm."

She immediately asks, "Solo, or accompanied?"

"Accompanied."

"Oh no. Didn't your family teach you how to use your gifts? What did the other person say?"

"He was really understanding and that kind of made it worse. My family heavily discourages the use of magic of any sort and, um, well. I'm not the kind of witch they like, anyway."

Falina had gone back to cleaning, but when I say that, she

spins around and says, "What do you mean, not the kind they like?"

"I sure hope you don't end up hating me about this. I'm a hybrid."

"Yes, duh. I told you I could smell that. I just don't recognize the other smell."

"The other smell is wolf."

"Get the fuck outta here. Really? You are a witch and a shifter? Wait, that's what they don't like?"

"Yes. My grandmother considers it to be a super shameful thing. She put a spell on my that only recently broke, to keep my wolf locked away from me."

"I don't like your family. I didn't realize I could dislike someone without ever meeting them, but I can smell the truth in what you are saying. So, I just want to go on record saying, fuck those assholes. I want you to meet my grandmother. She will not let you remain uneducated about using your gift. It really isn't safe. Jeez. Just, what the actual fuck? Leave a fire child untrained and lock away half of her?" Falina's rant subsides into angry mumbles as we get back to cleaning. I feel sorry for the dirt. She is going to annihilate it.

By the end of the day, she is happy again and as we are getting ready to head out, she tells me, "I sent a text to my grandma. She'd like to meet with you this weekend, if possible."

"Really? Ok. Um, is it ok if I bring my um… lover? I have to warn you, he is a sort of vampire. But he can't drink just anyone's blood."

"Gods, yes, my grandma is going to be so excited. We really only know witches. This is going to be great. Does he eat food? Like, not blood food?"

"Yes, he does actually."

"Fantastic. Come hungry, we are going to barbecue."

Chapter Eighteen

I've spent the week working with Falina, having runs every other night with the family, and spending as much time with Matthew as possible. I don't know if I am really his wife reincarnated, but time with him is healing me in ways I never expected or realized I needed. Sometimes I feel like maybe I am her, I just seem to know him or know some weird little thing about him. Maybe I should have asked the gods when they appeared in my room. I still can't believe I had gods in my room. Or that Odin is a perv who wanted to see my boobs.

This isn't what I need to think about right now. What I need to think about is meeting Falina's grandmother shortly and trying not to embarrass myself. What is she going to think about a witch with no training at all? Especially a hybrid witch? Will she feel the way my grandmother feels about it? Please, please, whatever gods listen to creatures like me, please let this go well. I need to know how to use my power and control it before I hurt someone by accident.

It doesn't take Matthew long to drive us to the address

Falina gave me. The house is one story, wooden and wide, set in a less urban space. They have more yard around their place than I am used to seeing. And so much greenery. I didn't realize it was possible to have a yard that looks like it was carefully planned and yet is so very wild. Before we get up the path from the driveway to the door, it flies open and Falina walks out to greet us. "Hello you two! Come on in! We have food going out back and grandma is waiting to meet you, Blaze." She hugs each of us as we draw near, then leads us into the house. Pointing towards the back of the house, she tells Matthew, "Just head that way. You'll find the back door and smell the food. Blaze, you're with me. Grandma is waiting in the spell closet." Matthew gives me an encouraging smile as he wanders off toward the back.

Falina leads me down a dark hallway that smells of incense and candles. A near the end stands open and light spills out into the hall. Falina knocks on the wall next to the door, waiting until a voice can be heard saying, "Come in, come in." She walks in and I follow her. I hear whispering voices as I cross the threshold. It's strange and unnerving, but I ignore it as best I can.

Inside the room is a woman older than me, though her seeming older is more about her presence than her looks. She and Falina look very similar. Red flowing hair, pale white skin that flushes even more easily than I do. But where the woman is tall and more thin, Falina is tall and voluptuous, with a more welcoming personality than the woman has displayed so far.

We both stop in front of her, a table between us and the woman. She turns her gaze on me and I want to squirm. It feels like she is reading my soul and it isn't the most comfortable thing ever. Then she frowns, "Oh child, I'm so sorry. You have nothing to be ashamed of. Lacking teaching is not a flaw. In your case, it is something we want to correct now, for exactly the reasons you worry about. And we will work on that. You and my granddaughter are going to do wonderful and terrible things. For today, we will content ourselves with learning how to maintain control when we are distracted by other things."

The heat of the blush makes me feel a little sweaty, but knowing that this woman probably read exactly what I was doing when I set fire to the bed is a little embarrassing. "Thank you, thank you so much. What do I do?"

She walks around the table and leads me to a circle painted on the floor that I had not noticed before now. Standing in the middle of the circle, I watch her walk around me, a shimmer falling from her fingertips. It touches the floor and spreads, closing in under my feet as well as rising to close over my head. When it is completely shielded, she stops in front of me. "Let it all out. Let the fire come out and just enjoy it for a little bit."

"What? I can't do that!"

"Why not? The shield will protect us, and you need to feel it release. You aren't going to be hurt by it, so set it free." Eyeing the shield around me, I try to do as she says. But I can't seem to let it go. "You can do this. Breathe, nice and deep, slow breaths. Let it out, feel the joy of releasing it intentionally."

She continues to talk, and her voice takes on a slightly hypnotic quality. I'm still fully aware, just less focused. The fire inside me wakes up, rising, curling in and flaring out. Sinuous and flickering as it travels. Letting it go is just such a relief. Such joy. I look down to see my hands are covered in flames. They are beautiful. Strange, but beautiful. I've never seen flames tinged with silver.

"Blaze," I look up from my hands in surprise. "It's time to

let it go rest. Ask your fire to curl back up inside you and wait for you to call it again."

I do as she says, but the fire doesn't go back to where it had been resting inside me. It wraps around me, flows through me. Flows through the wolf that is me now. It fills the space that is us and then rests while still being spread through us. My eyes fly open as I realize what must have happened. Looking at Falina's grandmother, I ask, "What was that?"

She smiles. "The last piece sliding into place. All you had to do was let go, trust it to do what it needed to do."

"But what did it need to do? I have an idea, but I would like you to say it out loud for me, please."

"It needed to join with you. What," she looks away briefly and takes a breath, "what your grandmother did should be punished. She split you into three pieces, and it not only harmed your mental health, it kept you weaker. Your power is going to grow over the course of the next week. You have magic on both sides of your family. The wolves on your father's side aren't just wolves. You aren't the first hybrid in that family. You will come back and I will help you to learn how to use your magic. For now, you have done enough. We are going out and join the family to eat and enjoy the afternoon."

"Before we go, what should I call you?"

She laughs, "I find that names are less important to me as I get older. My name is Glenda. You may call me grandma, like Falina does."

As I follow them out, I marvel at the ease with which this woman walks. Falina and I, we aren't what most would call young. I'm in my late forties and she is too. But this is her grandmother, and she has no issues walking. I felt her magic surrounding me as I worked. She doesn't even look tired and

I am over here feeling like I ran a marathon. "Can I ask a question before we get outside?"

They stop and turn to face me. "Of course. What is concerning you?"

"This is probably silly, but I was noticing you seem fine. Just as much energy as you had before we started. Meanwhile, I feel like I ran for miles. I'm drained. Why?"

Glenda chuckles. "What you did was a lot more work than what I did. And Falina helped me. You had only your own power, which had never truly been used. Escaped a few times, but never intentionally used. It's like a muscle. You have to use it or it atrophies. Have some food, you'll feel better after that."

"That makes a lot more sense than I ever expected from magic. Thank you."

My first lesson in using my power. Most of what happened was me letting it be part of me again. And now I have to go eat and try to be ok socializing with mostly, people I have never met. Honestly, I haven't even known Falina long.

Matthew spots me as soon as I step outside. His warm smile comforts me and the smell of the food on the grill has my stomach rumbling loudly. Falina turns and says, "Come on, I am taking you to the food right now. I don't care if it is done or not, you are eating now."

She threads her arm through mine and tugs me along with her across the lawn to where a man is standing at the grill. He is rocking a dad bod as he laughs and talks with some other people standing around him and the grill. Falina taps his arm. "Uncle Phil, she needs some food right now. She can't wait until it's all ready. Just a little plate will do, but she worked really hard in there with Grams and now she is depleted. Oh, and this is my friend, Blaze. Blaze, this is Uncle Phil."

He is filling a plate before she finishes her request and handing it over to me as she introduces us. "Nice to meet you, Blaze. It isn't fully done, but if you are what I think you are, slightly raw meat will not bother you."

I can't help but laugh. Slightly raw meat didn't bother me before I found out, and definitely less so now. "Thank you, I appreciate the food. You are probably right, but for now I have to go eat before I embarrass myself with how quickly I eat this."

They laugh and wave me off. As I turn, I see Matthew behind me. He murmurs, "There is a table just over here." he points to the right at a grouping of tables. One is still empty. Glenda is sitting at one, holding court with five other women. I head for the empty table with Matthew. He pulls out the chair for me. It is a strange experience to have someone just continuing to be nice to me. And right now, I have four people that have just been really awesome to me, with no relation or anything to gain. They just want to help me.

The food is helping, and I catch Glenda nodding at me in approval. Matthew says, "That the grandmother?"

"Yes, sorry, I forgot you didn't get to meet her."

"It's fine. I am not the priority here. The question is, did she help?"

"She did. She also told me things I was unaware of. For instance, my grandmother basically split me into three pieces to keep one side of me from ever showing up and embarrassing her. Which is why I had almost no control over my magic. I wasn't really connected to it. Now that I have had some food, I have to say, I feel… complete. Like, I don't recall ever having felt so together in my life. I feel competent. I know this probably sounds insane, especially since I have been taking care of myself for a long time, but I never felt like I was doing it right. And I think maybe I could now, if that makes sense."

"That makes a lot of sense. I don't know of anyone that would feel right split into three pieces. Are you going to keep learning from her?"

"I am. I think I need to. Because I have no doubt that my grandmother knows what happened. She isn't going to be happy about it."

Chapter Nineteen

MATTHEW

It has been a few weeks since the gods showed up in Blaze's room, and the others, like me, are working their way here from the various places they have been. The corruption is all over the world at this point, even if it seems that the focus will be here to start with. The church is expanding its reach massively. They have been buying up companies left and right, hell; they are even trying to force one of my companies to sell to them.

It isn't happening. They didn't do their research well enough. My company is much larger than it appears with a regular investigation. But, that they are trying to take over financially is more than a little concerning. No one needs a world in which the church is in control. And that is why I am meeting with the gods again. This time, they set a time and place instead of just popping in.

Pulling into the parking lot of one of my buildings, I notice a cloud sitting over my building, shading it. On an otherwise completely sunny day. I'm going to have to talk with them about this. Humans are going to notice.

Getting myself to the roof as quickly as possible, I start out with telling them, "You can't have a single large cloud to make it shady up here. You could have umbrellas up here, shade tarps, pavilions. Any number of things that aren't one cloud stationary over one building. The humans are going to be screaming about aliens."

Frigg and Freya both have smug looks on their faces, stares leveled at Odin. He looks sheepish as he claps his hands once. The cloud disperses and a large tent appears over us.

Sophia says, "I think we should get right to it. This isn't something we can wait on. Events are moving much faster than we expected."

"What events? Are we talking about the financial takeover that the church is working on? I have enough companies spread over the world to fight that. Easily."

Frigg turns her gaze out one of the doors. "No. It isn't that. It is so much bigger than just a financial takeover."

She glances at Freya, who picks up the thread. "They are drawing perilously close to creating a god of one of their preachers. The one you have been trailing. Did the others say how long before they would arrive?"

"Fen said he'll be here within the week."

Odin grumbles, "Fucking Fenrir. Of course he would get here first."

Keeping the smile off my face and out of my voice is not the easiest thing. Fen, being part of the group, has always been a source of irritation for Odin. Probably because Fenrir Grayback is fated to swallow Odin whole during the time of Ragnarok. Admittedly, Fen mentioning how hungry he is while staring pointedly at Odin every time they meet might have something to do with the irritation. "Yes, he is. The others were finishing things where they were. Fen said something about having gotten a bite to eat and finishing his job at the same time."

Frigg and Freya both have sudden coughing fits while Odin glares at them. Sophia says, "As entertaining as the talk of Fenrir eating Odin is, can we get back to the subject of these assholes pretending to follow my teachings while they strive to replace me?"

Odin looks relieved even as he intensifies his glower. "Yes. Let's try to stay on topic."

"I am curious as to why in the fuck you lot would even allow the raising of a human to godhood to even be a thing. I feel like you didn't really think that through."

Odin snorts. "I can assure you, it wasn't our fucking idea. Truth be told, this is how most of us came to be gods. It was accidental. We did things and collected worshippers by default of the times we lived in. The only ones that didn't start out that way are our children, like Freya here. She was born a goddess. Most of the rest of us were not. All the stories about the incest of the Greek pantheon, all false. Zeus, Poseidon, and Hades were never brothers in the way of being born family, they were warriors. That's why we are all so human, because we were. Zeus was always a shitty husband that cheated on Hera. None of us have been able to figure out why the hell she is still with him."

Hera appears behind Odin. "I'm just a glutton for punishment, perhaps. Or, perhaps I prefer him distracted while I tend to other things. Either way, it's none of your concern, Odin."

He flinches at the sound of her voice. "Sorry about that Hera, it's just that Zeus's behavior is such a prime example."

She looks down her nose at him. "You could always just talk about how your blood-thirst elevated you to godhood."

"Not everyone is comfortable with that, Hera."

"I'm comfortable with it." Odin's narrowed eyes and lips pressed together so hard his beard swallows them entirely tell me that now is the time to remember that I am not actually a god. "Moving on. How close are we talking? And what does it mean, that he is getting close to being a god? Is he marveling at strange new powers already? Or anticipating some ritual to seal the deal?"

Sophia grimaces. "Both. He is gaining in abilities that he is using in the most atrocious manner possible—"

"It turns even my stomach to see it," Odin says, looking uncharacteristically somber.

She continues, "And he has created a ritual to seal the deal. Normally, that would do nothing. But, as he will have the power of belief behind it, along with the majority of my followers, once he does that, we won't be able to take it from him."

Hera walks over and puts an arm around Sophia. "Worse yet, that will take enough of Sophia's followers to have a dire effect on her."

"What could possibly be dire for you all?"

Freya says quietly, "If you weren't born a god, you only stay a god so long as people believe in you. His concentrated attack on the belief in her will rob her of her godhood eventually, if it doesn't happen when he becomes a god. And with her gone, the others will not be far behind." She hugs Frigg, tears running down her face unchecked. "We are going to win if I have to kill him myself."

Frigg hugs her back, murmuring, "You can't. I won't have your life lost to interference with humans. We cannot directly interfere. We will simply have to win."

"I didn't realize the stakes were that high. We'll find a way. Is there anything else we need to know?"

Odin walks over, pulls out a knife and slices his thumb.

Touching the bloody thumb to my forehead, he whispers something in a language I don't understand. "This will protect you from his power. The others will get the same. Except Fenrir. He'll get it from someone, not me."

I can feel a strange tickle on my forehead as he steps away. Jokes about why Odin would not want to be protecting Fenrir cross my mind, as does the reminder that I am not a god. Keeping the latter part firmly in the forefront of my thoughts helps me keep any jokes that ma get me killed sealed away. Freya has a glint in her eye like she can see what I am thinking and her smirk says I'm not wrong.

Sophia says, "Yes. That mark will only protect you from so much. And the more people that see you fight, the more that become firm believers in his power, the more powerful he will become. You want him isolated and you all need to take him out quick. Once he is dead, burn his body and scatter the ashes far and wide. We don't want him becoming some tale of resurrection."

"Why is that even possible? Who is making these rules? Can we negotiate with them? Beat some sense into them?"

Freya laughs, "Technically, human belief in resurrection stories are what made it possible. So, yes and no. You could, but it wouldn't help."

"Of fuckin' course it wouldn't. Ok. Is there anything else?"

The gods start to disappear before my eyes. Except Hera. She stands still, watching. I understand now why her symbolism has to do with the eyes on peacock feathers. When everyone has gone, she says, "What are your plans for Blaze?"

I have a sudden feeling like my life is hanging in the balance of what I say. My heart beats fast and I work to swallow the lump of fear that is suddenly lodged in my throat. "I would like to be hers as long as she wants me, and I plan to do everything in my power to keep her wanting me. If for some reason she chooses differently, I won't like it. At all. But I will continue to protect her, from afar if necessary."

She nods, walking in a slow circle around me. "And what if she takes a new lover? What then?"

"I hate it and continue to protect her. And him as applies to keeping her safe. But I'm not extending myself extra for him."

She chuckles as she comes to a stop in front of me. "Good. I want her safe. And free to choose as she will. You work at not constraining her choices. She will need to know she has your support, even when you don't agree with her."

A terrible suspicion is snaking its way through my mind. "Why? Why does she need to be free to choose even when I disagree? What is this about, Hera?"

Her eyes narrow, and I feel certain she is thinking about hitting me. "Because it is her actions that will change the world. You men are so full of yourselves. Running about, certain that you are the be all, end all. That isn't the case. It never was. Women have always been the change the world needs. Women have always been the embodiment of a power that terrifies weak men. Blaze needs support to become," she pokes me in the chest, "if you cannot be that support, I will send her someone that can. She is special to me. I will see her reach her full potential even if you have to get out of her way. Make your choice." she waves her arm off to the right and shadow figures appear. They aren't clear, being smoky images, but her message is crystal clear.

"I choose to support her however she needs, even if I don't agree with her choices."

She smiles and the smoky figures disappear. "Good boy. Now, run along. You have things to do."

I watch as she disappears before I turn and head for the first floor and my car. They left the damn pavilion up here. I'm going to have to send some people up to get rid of it.

* * *

Blaze

The house is beautiful. And Frankie loves how close it is to her. She and Falina have really hit it off since they met here today and I am so glad my friends like each other. They both love the idea of me in this house and, if I'm honest, so do I. Glenda owns it and she didn't want to take any money, swearing that having it not sitting vacant would ease her mind greatly.

I talked her into taking some money, but it is still such a small amount. Falina and Frankie come walking back in, having left me alone to get the feel of the house. Falina says, "So, what's your decision? You feel like a decision made. What have you decided?"

Turning around in a circle one more time to look at the place, I stop facing them. "I'm going to take it. I don't see how I could say no. Fuck, I love this place already and I haven't been here for an hour."

"Grandma had a feeling you were who this place had been waiting for. And we are all living near each other!" Frankie grins. "What do you say to another girl's night? With maybe only one kind of wine, that mixing of wines last time hurt the next morning."

"I say, what better way to celebrate my first weekend home?"

Squeals of joy and celebration commence as we hug and talk excitedly about how I am going to decorate the place. Falina chimes in, "Grandma said if you take the place she will be here tonight to cast spells with us for—"

Frankie interjects, "Cast spells?"

Falina looks confused. "I thought with the way you had the air currents moving with you that you knew?"

Realization dawns on me, and a smile grows across my face. "Frankie! You're a witch too? Did you not know either?"

Frankie is looking scared. "I don't know what you're talking about. What do you mean, the air currents around me?"

Falina's hand covers her mouth. The horror on her face is painful to see. I take Frankie by the arm and lead her over to a wall to sit. This way, she has something to lean on if she feels weak when she figures it out. "Come, let's sit down and talk about it. If you had no idea, then we should be sitting to discuss it."

Frankie lets me lead her and Falina follows, apologizing profusely. "I am so sorry. It never occurred to me to keep my mouth shut. I just thought you knew. I mean, Blaze knew, she just didn't have any training. But I thought you had training. Ah hell."

We all get settled in and Falina continues, "Frankie, I don't know why you don't know you are magical, but you most assuredly are. And I am going to tell you the same as I would anyone. You need to know how to control your power. It would really suck if you drew in a tornado because you were feeling especially awful about a breakup or something, you know?"

Falina is about to say more when Frankie holds up her hand, palm out. "Wait. I need to make sure I am not hearing things. Did you really just say I am magic?" Falina and I both nod in agreement. "So all the times that I heard things whispered in the wind, all the times that I swore to my mother that the wind was listening, all the times she said I was crazy;

it was all lies? I really do have magic? You aren't fucking with my head or some damn hallucination?"

Falina looks at me and back to Frankie. "I don't know what the hell is wrong with your families. Frankie, it was all lies. You are as magical as the day is long." She reaches over and pinches Frankie. "And this isn't a hallucination. You both have incredibly shitty families that would treat you this way and if I ever meet them, I'm going to tell them all to kick rocks. Ooo. I have to go outside for a little bit. Just knowing your families are out there being assholes to you both pisses me off. I'm walking up to Grandma's. It'll burn off the energy. Follow when you are ready. She is going to want to talk to you too, Frankie."

We watch in silence as this beautiful, curvy woman stomps out of the house with her red, curly hair flowing behind her. The entire house shakes a little as she stomps. I guess she really is angry. Standing, I walk over to the door she left open. The cracks in the sidewalk are blooming dandelions behind her and next to it little rocks are coming up out of the ground. I find I am a little comforted that I am not the only one that leaks magic when I am troubled. Shutting the door, I go sit down beside Frankie. She's been quiet and staring into the distance since Falina cleared the door. "So, how's your brain?"

She chuckles. "I think it may be less broken than it has been in a long time." She looks at me with tears in her eyes. "I thought I was crazy. My family had me hiding myself even from them and, unless I am some strange anomaly, they knew I wasn't crazy. This, this makes everything they did and said when I got pregnant and after I had my son, just, it's so much worse."

She is sitting cross-legged and leaned forward so I throw an arm around her and hug her to me. Then, because I want to make her laugh, I pull up a tiny fireball in my hand and make it look similar to a cartoon flame shaking its butt. She laughs. "When did you find out about this?"

"I've known all my life, but my grandma hated me for being a dirty mixed blood and she split me into three parts. I have always struggled to contain the fire. Until we go everything in me merged, I spent my life terrified I would burn the world down. I guess while we are talking about things you didn't know, the hybrid part is because I am what most people would call a werewolf. Except I have more control than that."

She nods, her head moving on my shoulder. "I'm not even surprised. I knew a wolf family once. They moved away after my mother caught me playing with one of them in their wolf form. I think my mom made them move."

"Well, she isn't in control of you anymore. Now, let's go follow the dandelion path and introduce you to grandma. She's probably going to adopt you, too."

* * *

* * *

I make it back to Matthew's hotel well after dark. I think I put it off because I don't want to see him hurt when I tell him I got my own place. What if he gets mad? Wait. This is Matthew. Even if he gets mad, he isn't going to hurt me over it. With my courage gathered up in both hands, I head for my room. The elevator doors open and I look at the two doors. I can't just wait for him to come over. Moving toward his door takes a lot, because it would be so much easier to grab my stuff, leave, and send him a text. Later. But that would definitely make me the asshole, and that's not who I want to be. He appears almost instantly after I knock, takes one look at my face and says, "Come in and tell me about it."

Why was this so scary? I know he isn't James. He keeps

showing he isn't and yet, my brain has trouble with the idea that he won't be similar. He walks over to the couch, and seating himself, he pats the other seat. I cross the room and sit down, and my brain short circuits. Everything pours out all at once.

"I got a new place. It's really close to where Frankie lives and Falina lives close, too. The houses belongs to her grandmother, and it feels like home and I don't know why. But I love it and I can afford it. She is barely letting me pay her anything, which is great because I don't really have a whole lot. And I don't want to hurt your feelings, but I need to have my own space that I pay for and it makes me feel bad to keep mooching off you—"

He stops the torrent with the simple expedient of putting a finger on my lips. "It's ok, Blaze. I understand. My only question is, does this mean you don't want to see me anymore?" He moves his hand away after he finishes his question.

"What? Oh! No! It doesn't mean that at all. I would love to continue seeing you. I just don't want to mooch off of you, or feel like I am even if you don't see it that way."

"Then all is well in my world. And I have some news that I see as good. The actual house I stay in when I am here isn't far from Frankie's house. So you live near me too."

"Really?"

"Yes. So, tell me about your house."

I spend what seems like hours telling him about this quaint Victorian house that my newly adoptive grandmother insists I help her with by living there. I love it so much and I've only spent a short amount of time in it. As I trail off the description, I notice a set of peacock feathers sticking out of a previously empty vase. "Those are pretty. Where'd you get them?"

He turns to see what I am referring to and snarls. "It's a reminder from one of the gods. I'm sure they think they are hilarious."

"Ok, I don't think I need to know more than that. You can have your inside jokes with them. I'll stay in a less complicated place where I don't really have much to do with them." He laughs when I say that and I tip my head, giving him a have you lost your mind look.

He gets himself together and says, "Those are about you. They aren't an inside joke. They are Hera's way of letting me know she is watching, always. She likes you. Your ability to not have much to do with them is zero. They, or at least one of them, are having much to do with you." My heart sinks. I feel like I just got free of a church and I don't want to go back. I don't want another pushy religion telling me how awful I am and how I will be going to some hell for how I was created. "What's wrong? You suddenly look like you just got dumped by your best friend."

"I was just thinking that I don't want to be sucked into a whole 'nother religion. I just got out. It just doesn't seem fair."

"Oh, I don't think that is really something you need to worry about. With the old gods, it is more like entering into a relationship. They can be pushy, and sometimes will manipulate circumstances to push you where you need to be, but overall they aren't bad to work with in that respect. My relationship is unique because I work for them. And we have had hundreds of years to build our relationship. They have appeared in my room many times over the years and I didn't mind because it was just me. I think they will concern themselves with whether or not you are there more, as they know it bothers you now. I think perhaps they forgot that not everyone is ok with them appearing in their bedroom while they are sleeping."

"That sounds better than a whole religion with rules and rude people. But, I don't know. It still feels like I don't have a choice."

"You can always say no. Hera isn't a monster. She isn't even the way they depict her in the mythos. I think you will probably like her once you get to know her. I can't say for certain, but my guess is that the reason she hasn't already introduced herself is to allow you time to adjust and get used to the idea of the old gods still wandering about."

"Maybe it will be all right? I'll figure that out later. Right now, I just want to get some sleep. I plan to take my things to the car in the morning. Would you maybe want to spend the night with me? I'll give you my new address now, so you'll know where to find me."

"Thank you. That will make it a faster trip to get to you. I'll have my things packed and sent to my house tomorrow. For now, how about we order in some dinner? Unless you would like to be dinner now?"

I can feel my cheeks heating as his eyes drift downward, and his meaning becomes crystal clear. "Um, possibly dinner and then the uh, other? Glenda put us through our paces today and I kind of need the fuel before I am super active again."

He laughs. "I'll order us a large meal, then."

Chapter Twenty

* * *

The weekend has arrived, finally. My stuff is still everywhere. Matthew's insane amount of money did really help me to not have to start from nothing again, and he does not know why I am so grateful. He simply doesn't understand being broke as fuck. But I remember when I first left my parents. It was hard and I don't want to go back to that place again. Shaking off the melancholy those kinds of thoughts bring in, I start working in the living area. At the very least, we have to have one clear room to enjoy while we have our very first girls' night for the three of us, and the first one in this house.

Falina and Frankie show up at the same time, knocking on the door as I am tossing a pile of clothing into my closet. I can hear them talking outside. Kicking the trailing bits into the closet, I head for the door. Throwing it open and welcoming them in, they hug me and tell me how nice the place looks as they come in.

"I picked up some food from Naan, if you all want to eat first?"

Frankie says, "I love that place. I thought I was smelling it as I walked up. Please, let's eat now."

The kitchen is in better shape, as I have been using it more and putting stuff away when I am in there. They settle in around the table as I grab the food out of the oven where I put it to stay warm.

We are happily eating and talking when it appears. Falina is the first to see it and she screams. An image of Pastor Ward's head is hanging in the air over our food. We scramble away from the table, the three of us gathering in front of the counter. "What are you doing here?"

The head laughs. "Watching over one of my flock that has strayed far from her path. James is waiting for you, you should go home to him. Bring your friends here to the church with you. We'll welcome them too."

"Absolutely not! You get out of my house!"

Falina is the one that grabs our hands and whispers, "Shields up and expand. We are pushing him out."

We do as she says, as Grandma Glenda taught us. Our shielding is meshed together, connected like our hands. As we push it out, he begins to shout. I can't pay attention to what he is saying or I will be the weak link. Falina speaks low and guides us through the setting of the shields so we don't have to focus on them to maintain them. The very instant she tells us we can let go now, tears start pouring down my face. "How did he find me?"

Frankie, out of breath like she ran a mile, asks, "Who the hell was that?"

"Pastor Ward. James works with him as a deacon. They are awful little peas in a pod."

Falina says, "Ok. Well, that is a horrifying new way to

recruit people. I have to say it is also the most invasive and I am really curious about how he managed it. I'm calling Grandma, she's going to have the entire family here to ward your house against fucking weirdos. Are you guys still hungry or should we toss what's left? I don't think I am going to be able to eat food from Naan for a little while without seeing that head over my food." She shudders even as Frankie and I both agree. The food has to go. The idea of it kind of turns my stomach right now. Which makes me a little more angry at Pastor Ward. Naan has superb food, but now him being a creeper is associated with it and I can't eat it with the picture of his head floating over us running through my mind.

I can hear Falina's end of the conversation with Glenda. I can only imagine what the other end sounds like. She has it pressed tight to her ear, muffling what sound does come through. If I had to guess, Falina isn't wrong in her initial assessment of what is about to happen. Swallowing down the lump in my throat, I start picking up the food and tossing it into the trash. As I am tossing in the last bit, I hear the front door opening. Fear grips me for a second until the sounds of Falina's family reach my ears. Frankie and I exchange a glance before getting ourselves out there with everyone else as quickly as possible.

Glenda sits us down and all the women in the family listen as we explain what happened. Glenda puffs up a little with what looks like pride as we tell them about Falina, guiding us through the shielding. Her face is grim once we have finished telling her who he is. "A pastor shouldn't be able to do that. There are a great many witches that could, and a great many other types of being that could. However, a human pastor should not be able to do that. He will bear watching. For now, we are simply going to add to your shield, and that should keep you for tonight."

Chapter Twenty-One

MATTHEW

The day has been long and as much as I miss having Blaze in the next room; it is really nice to see my house again. An old woman wanders into the yard from the neighbor's side yard as I pull into the drive. Maybe she is lost. Getting out of my car, I nudge the door closed and walk toward her. "Excuse me, are you lost? Do you need help?"

She looks up at me. Something strange about her eyes. "I do need help. I'm sure you can help me, big, strong man like you." Even as I take a step back from her, her hands come up and something shoots out of her hands. It hits my head, and the world goes dark as I fall to the ground.

* * *

Blaze

Work was a beast today. So many people, so many of them women, in one night. It made for today being really busy as we started the work of getting them ready for their final resting. Pulling into my driveway is kind of awesome. Before I get out, I try Matthew's phone again. I haven't heard from him since yesterday and it is a little weird. I don't think

I should worry too much, but all the same I find I am worried. Shoving the phone in my purse after it goes to voicemail again, I get out of the car. Before I unlock my door, I see an envelope on the step. I look around to see if anyone is near before I pick it up.

Using a key to open it, I pull out the heavy paper inside.
* * *

We have Matthew. Come to the church ready to marry James or Matthew dies. If you marry him and leave quietly for your honeymoon, we will set him free before you board the plane. We expect you before seven pm.
* * *

The paper begins to smoke and I drop it along with everything else in my hands. The fury in me knows no bounds and I can't decide if I want to howl out my fury before I go rip out their throats in my wolf form or burn the fucking church to the ground. No, I want Matthew back, dammit. He is mine. No one gets to take him from me. Pulling the flames back in allows me to pull my phone out of my purse. I call Frankie first.

"Hey Blaze, got to keep it quick. I'm at work."

"They took Matthew. Can you come help?"

"Where are you? I'll be there shortly."

I tell her I am at my house as she hollers to someone that she has to go now. She says, "Wait there," and hangs up the phone.

I call Falina next. "Blaze, what's up?"

"They took Matthew. Will you help me get him back?"

"Are you at your house?"

"Yes."

"I'll run down now."

"Maybe stay out of the road. Frankie is on her way."

"Got it."

She ends the call, and I let my phone drop back into my purse. Standing, I pace the little walk as I wait for them. If I go in there, all the focus will be on me. Which means they can get him out safely before I turn the place into ashes. They'll have to call me or something. Maybe they can throw a rock through one of the windows? That would be nice to see.

Falina runs into the yard. "How did you find out they have him?"

I point at the lightly charred note on the ground near my purse. She picks it up and gasps as she reads it. "You aren't going to marry him, are you?"

I laugh as Frankie screeches to a halt in front of the house. She is out of the car and running across the yard before the engine is fully off. "Where did they take him?"

Falina hands her the note. She crumbles it after reading it. "You aren't marrying that prick."

"No. But I'm going to go in and keep them focused on me while you two go get Matthew. There are cages in the basement. I always thought it was strange. Why have cages in a church? But I would bet that is where they have him at. If not, then after I burn the church to the ground, we'll check the pastor's house."

Falina and Frankie exchange a glance, shrug, and Frankie asks, "We taking your car or mine?"

"Mine. You'll both have to lie down in the back. They can't see you with me."

We pile into the car and I get us headed towards the church. As I drive, I tell them, "Don't worry about fingerprints or dna. The fire will erase that. But if you could make sure that no cameras nearby see us, that would be great."

Frankie chuckles, "I swear that old woman has precog.

Yes, I got this." She is silent for the last few minutes of the drive. As I park up close to the church, for the first time, she says, "I got them. Since it was the wind that pushed them, I doubt anyone will bother with them till tomorrow."

Looking at the building, I murmur, "Good. Put a rock through the window or something to let me know when you all are out of the building."

They agree as I get out and head for the doors.

Chapter Twenty-Two

M ATTHEW

Where the fuck am I? What did that woman hit me with? I don't smell anyone in here with me, so I open my eyes. The ceiling is concrete. No windows. Three walls are concrete, the floor feels like I am laying on concrete, and the last wall is bars. Sitting up feels unpleasant, and I can't help but wonder again, what the fuck did that woman hit me with?

Paying more attention to the smells, I realize I am in the church and those bars are electrified. Fuck me, that's not good. Do they know? Do they know why I am here? How could they find out about the mission? Do they have Blaze? What about Fen? I haven't heard from him. Are they the reason for that? I hear a noise outside the room. It sounds like someone trying to be quiet. Laying back down on the floor, I wait as I hear doors open and close, while the person gets closer. The door creaks open and I hear steps, mostly silent but audible to my ears. Their scent drifts in and my eyes fly open. "Falina?"

"Shh!!! Jesus, why are you so fucking loud?"

I want to laugh, but if she is here, then Blaze is, too. And she is in danger just for being in the vicinity of James. "Where is Blaze?"

"Upstairs, trying to hold off on turning this place into a charcoal briquette until we are out. Any idea where the keys are for your fancy little holding cell?"

"No, I haven't been awake very long."

"Hm, ok. Uh, maybe step back a few steps." I move back one step because I can float and she shrugs before focusing on the floor. A circle, maybe four feet wide, opens up under the bars. Letting myself dissolve into smoke, I flow through the hole and out to the other side. As I reform on solid ground, Falina says, "Why did I need to make a hole if you could turn to smoke? You could have gone through the bars and saved me the trouble of trying to do that quietly. Do you have any idea how difficult it is to move rock quietly?"

"No, but the bars are electrified. It would have been really painful to go through them."

"Ok, we need to get outside. She sounded really serious about setting fire to this place. And that pastor really needs some hell fire."

My fangs descend. "The good pastor is out there? You know, I'm feeling peckish. Are you good to get out of here? I have a stop to make."

"Oh shit, you're gonna bite the pastor? I want to see it. I'm coming with you."

"I plan to move fast. Let me carry you."

She grimaces. "I'll slow you down. Maybe just go ahead and I'll catch up. I'm sure I won't miss much."

"What the hell kind of men have you all been around that they can't handle you? Fucking hell. I'm carrying you. You aren't going to slow me." I have scooped her up before she can say anything else and am running for the upstairs. In the hall, my brain applies where I am to the map of this place in my head. Heading back the way she came, I move fast enough that Falina is pressed into my chest. The landing at the top of the stairs is a wide, open area, so I stop and set her down. I can smell them in the other room, smell my Blaze. Falina is a little dizzy, but waves me on as she creeps along with one hand on the wall.

"Don't go in for a couple of minutes. I'm going to enter from the other side. I want that pastor."

* * *

Blaze

Entering the church, I know exactly where they will be. The main nave, likely actually the sanctuary as they both prefer not to mingle overmuch in the 'common' area, as they call it. Pushing through the doors, I see James and a different pastor in the sanctuary. I don't know this one at all, not that it matters. "James, what the hell are you thinking? Kidnapping? Really?"

James snorts. "Get over here. You don't know what you're talking about. He isn't human. Human laws don't apply to him." Fuck, they know what he is? How did they find out? "Unless, of course, you are ready for him to die. We can go ahead and do that. Pastor Gant, go—"

"No! Wait. I'm coming. Who is this pastor?" I ask as I walk toward him. "Why isn't Pastor Ward here?"

"You are going to learn to live in silence now that we will be married. I can't have my wife asking so many tiresome questions. But I'll indulge you on your wedding day since you won't have a dress and I know how important that type of thing is to you women. Pastor Ward is at a meeting with the heads of the church organization." He reaches out and grabs my arm, pulling me to his side and crushing me to him.

I allow it, because I haven't heard a window break yet and I need to keep him distracted. Even so, I can feel my temperature rising, the fire in me restless to burn the fingers of this shit that dares to touch me again after putting me in the hospital.

Think Blaze, what will keep him talking? I look up for inspiration and I see Frankie in the fucking rafters. I cough to cover my noise of surprise. James slaps my back much harder than necessary and I refrain from straightening to punch him is his smug fucking face.

Pastor Gant clears his throat. "Excuse me, we need to get on with this. I have a warm bed to get to and I would much prefer to be there."

James grabs my arms, snatching me up against him. "Ready to get married, my little Bea?"

We hear a gurgle from the pastor and I turn to find Matthew, his lips clamped on the pastor's neck and drinking deep. I'm oddly turned on by the sight and have to remind myself to focus as James cries out, "What the hell? Help!"

Before he can drag me off anywhere, I reach between us and grab his dick, twisting it viciously. He releases me, and tries to slap me but, I'm a lot stronger now that all of me is incorporated. Blocking his swing, I give his parts a yank before I let go and punch him in the face. He falls to the ground, clutching himself as he struggles to call for help. Unfortunately, his call for help was heard. The doors on either side of the nave are thrown open, men rushing in. Until they fly back, hitting the walls hard and slumping to the floor. Frankie comes floating down, landing lightly next to James. She kicks him in the gut before she turns to me. "I think it might be time to go?"

Matthew drops the lifeless body of Pastor Gant. "I think now is a good time to leave."

The men on either side of the room start to get up but fall screaming when the floor opens underneath them. Their screams echo in the nave. Falina calls across the nave, "So, are we going, or did you plan to wait for reinforcements?"

Matthew says, "I need to make a quick side trip. You still plan to let this place burn to the ground, right?"

"Yes, I want them to understand I do not belong to them and I will burn down everything they love if they continue on this mission to force me to marry this asshole."

Matthew snarls down at James, kneeling down. He whispers something that has James whimpering. "I'll see you outside, ok?" I nod and he reaches out, his hand cupping my cheek briefly and then he is gone. Nothing but a breeze and the ghost of his hand on my cheek to show he was ever here. Well, if you ignore the body of Pastor Gant.

Falina says, "Should we make sure there aren't any bodies?"

I look at her. "You can do that?"

She shrugs. "It is fairly easy to bury them under the church. Anyone else in here can evacuate when the building is catching fire."

"Yes, do it."

Frankie tips her head at James as he tries to crawl away. "What do we want to do with him? Maybe Falina could drop him down with the rest of them?"

James starts crying and wets himself. "No, I think letting him live will be the proper punishment here. Let him crawl away, knowing that I hurt him and put him on the ground. He'll never tell anyone for fear that his shame will be revealed. Because it will. I will tell everyone. I might take out a billboard. The members of the church will have to see it every time they come to church."

He cries harder and we turn back to Falina. She is

waiting, arms crossed and foot tapping. "Are we done taunting the weak man? We need to go."

I look around, and I spot an ancient lamp on the piano. They only have it because the old man that plays it insists that it is the only one that works with his eyes. Reaching out toward it, I let a few little licks of flame play around the plug. Melting it and starting a small fire that will rage very soon.

We walk out slowly, as though nothing unusual has happened. Frankie and Falina get in the back seat, and not long after, Matthew appears next to the car. Holding a mini pc and a small bag of jump drives. Once he is in, I back out of the spot and start to drive away when an image of Pastor Ward appears in front of us. "I'll see you soon, little girl."

I hate his fucking face. I drive through his image and I am pretty satisfied when he dissipates.

Chapter Twenty-Three

As we drive away, things start to settle in and I realize I've made an enemy of a man with a lot of power, both socially and magically. "Falina, is your grandma up at this time of night?"

She laughs, "Yes. Grandma isn't much for sleeping at night. Why?"

"I think we need to talk to her. Pastor Ward is really mad. And James obviously has a vendetta, leaving him alive might have been a mistake."

"We could go find him and fix that. I wouldn't mind another snack." The car is silent for a moment as we all process what Matthew said. Frankie is the first one to start laughing. It's infectious and we all end up laughing as I drive.

Matthew just looks confused till I explain, "We are all just entertained at the idea of turning around so you could have a little James snacky. It's probably a stress thing. I don't know that is really a good plan. So, we are going to go talk to Glenda and get some advice from her."

Falina sends a text to Glenda that we are descending upon her, she sends a thumbs up in return. We arrive just a few minutes later and somehow, Glenda already has tea ready for all of us. And cookies. Witches love cookies. Once she knows why we are there, she asks for the entire story and we share it all. Even the bits I am not excited to share. When we have finished, she turns to Matthew. "You said an older woman hit you with something. What was it?"

"I don't know. She didn't seem to have anything in her hands…"

Realization dawns on us all. Pastor Ward is working with witches. Witches are helping him. I look at Matthew. "You have to tell us what else is going on."

He nods. "I'm going to have to call them in. They need to be part of this conversation, too."

A woman's voice comes from behind me. "We have been watching this develop. He is careful to never meet with the witches in person, which is why, until you were taken, we didn't know about the connection. That and, frustratingly enough, much of what he does we can't see. Now that we know he is working with witches, we can work at more effectively breaking through that."

I turn to see who is behind me, and immediately I know she is a goddess. She has that same other quality to her that the ones I met that morning in my room at Matthew's hotel. She isn't one of them, though. Her dress is more modern, even with all the feathers hanging from it. Feathers… Peacock feathers. Oh. This is Hera. A little gasp of surprise draws her attention to me, and she smiles. Holy shit. I try to smile back, because what can you do when a goddess smiles at you? I sure as hell don't want to piss her off.

Glenda says, "He's been working with you all this time?"

Hera's lips drop at the corners. "No, not really. I've kept

an eye on things, but Sophia is the ringleader for the circus he is in."

Matthew snorts, and I look at him in amazement. He shrugs, saying, "The shock and awe go away after a hundred years or so."

Hera raises a brow. "Faster, even if you start out mad at the gods because your wife was murdered while you fought a holy war for a church that claimed to be doing the will of god."

Matthew looks away. "If any of them are ever reincarnated, I hope I get to see them one. Last. Time." His fist is clenched on his thigh and I reach over to cover it with my hand. His hand relaxes and turns up to hold mine. Hera smiles down at it. "Fen will be here soon." She looks at the group, "They are worried only about the church, focused on the one pastor." Her eyes focus on me. "They didn't notice the witch collecting power. But they didn't notice her as she hid in plain sight, nothing but another socialite ruling over her family with an iron fist to maintain her standing. They didn't notice the way she was pulling strings everywhere."

I feel like my heart is going to beat right out of my chest. I know she's talking about my grandmother. Holy shit, she is terrifying. I don't really want to fight her. She split me into three pieces. But shit, what if she ends up in control? Oh fuck me, that can't happen. "She isn't the problem yet. But she will be. She is why you will need an army. She isn't working alone. Let Matthew and the team he is working with handle Pastor Ward. You witches are going to need to stop her."

Glenda asks, "Why us? Why don't you just smite her or something?"

Hera rolls her eyes. "Because we aren't allowed to do that sort of thing anymore. Between all the rapes and the wars started and the general fuckery, the universe decided it had quite enough shenanigans from the ones it assigned to watch over the humans. Thus, we are now constrained from direct interference. We can assemble teams, we can tell you where to go and how to get there. We can use subtle influence to move things the way we feel is best. But we cannot simply slap some sense into someone."

Glenda nods. "I thought as much. Very well. That's why the church got so bad, eh? A witch war. I hoped to never see one in my time."

"The gift of time to prepare is one I am able to give. I will be watching over you all. Especially you, Blaze."

"Um, thanks? It's my grandmother, isn't it?"

"It is."

"I guess at least now I know why."

"Oh no, you know part of the reason why. When you have fully stepped into your power, then you will know why she wanted you broken. Why she still wants you broken."

Chapter Twenty-Four

BLAZE

It all seems surreal. I haven't even told my brother what happened. Or my aunt. Shit. I still forget that I have this whole other family. Sometimes it still surprises me when one of them shows up for a night run. I need to go spend some time with them soon. I feel like they could help with the war and I just don't know how. A peacock feather appears on my sink. Hera keeps leaving these everywhere, so I know she is watching over me. I am guessing she hasn't realized it might get a little much, eventually. Especially if she is going to toss these out while I am in the bathroom getting ready for a date.

I need to think about this date. Not all the other stuff. Just focus on this for this one evening. Hera said, we have time, and Matthew's friend Fen hasn't even arrived yet.

Whatever happens, if I answer the door in my underwear, we aren't going out. I'm wearing pants tonight. A dress is more than I can deal with right now. I know putting on makeup first is a dumb idea, but here we are doing it, anyway. I'll just be extra careful when I put on the shirt.

Thirty minutes later, I hear Matthew knocking on the door

and I am still in my underwear. Shit. Dashing to my closet, I grab a pair of pants, stretchy but not casual looking. Top. I need a shirt. Fuck. I grab a shirt and quickly shove my arms through, grateful it's a button up. Buttoning the shirt as I walk, I finish just as I get to the door. Opening it, I step back and invite Matthew in. He chuckles as he walks past. "You might want to have a second go at buttoning that shirt, or let me help you with it. We aren't making it to dinner on time if I help you."

Confused, I look down and see that small children are better at buttoning their shirts than I am. I push the door closed as I hurry to the bedroom, calling over my shoulder, "I'll be ready shortly."

It doesn't take me very long to get the shirt buttoned properly. Shoes, that takes a minute. I eventually settle on some black flats just because I am still feeling too anxious for heels.

Back in the living area, he is waiting. Gods, he is gorgeous. I still worry that one day he'll find the woman that was his wife and he'll leave me, but I'm going to enjoy this as long as I can. Matthew reaches out and takes my hand, pulling me to him. His arms wrapping around me as he releases my hand, "Are you ready to go or do you want to stay here and think of something else to do? You seem nervous?"

Snuggling into his chest, I tell him, "I am. Nervous, that is. Not about you, just everything else. Pastor Ward. My grandmother. Whoever she is working with. I'm worried for us, for our friends, for my newly found family. What if—"

His hands go to my shoulders, gently pushing me back so he can see my face. "Listen to me. You are strong and you are not alone. Besides, I've waited hundreds of years to find you again. I will cheerfully tear into pieces anyone that hurts you and then we can dance on the pieces. Love, you just burnt a church to the ground. I saw the news. They couldn't put the flames out until the entire church was nothing but ashes. I know you didn't do that because you were mad they tried to force you to marry him. You were mad that they took me and you came there with the intention that you were going to leave that place in flames. I have no doubt that you will protect everyone you love. Not to mention, none of us are exactly defenseless. Your family is literally a bunch of wolves. And your friends are all witches. I've got a bite that kills and supernatural strength. And my friends are way the fuck out there. Wait till you meet Fen."

"What is Fen?"

"Did you ever read the old Norse stories about Odin?"

"Yes, mythology is fascinating. I read about a lot of different mythos."

"Did you read the part about the wolf, Fenrir?"

"Yes, the whole story was pretty fucking tragic for the wolf. Like, why jump right into chaining him up? Why not be his friend, earn his loyalty?"

"Odin isn't real big on earning things like loyalty. He prefers that people earn his favor. And he is incredibly superstitious. A seer tells him something, and he is certain that is how it will be. No matter that they tell him, the future is not certain. So he gets a premonition from somewhere and acts on it. Which is how Fen ended up in chains for a very long time. He still isn't Odin's biggest fan."

"Wait, your friend Fen is Fenrir? The Fenrir? Fenrir, that is supposed to eat Odin at some point?"

"The very one."

"And he isn't in chains anymore?"

"Not for a very long time. Frigg is less superstitious than he is and when this war started, she talked him into it. Fen is really quite fond of her. I think she may be the only reason he doesn't bite Odin every time he sees him."

My stomach rumbles before I can say anything. "I think maybe we should get going?"

He laughs. "It would seem so."

We get going and he is slowing to stop for a light when he says, "That's her!"

"Her?" I look, and there is an older woman crossing the street in front of us. "Who is she?"

"That's the woman that hit me with something before I woke up in the church."

Even as he speaks, her hands lift from her sides and she fires at the car. Everything under the hood explodes, the hood itself smashing the windshield and blocking our view of her. The fire in me is in my hands, begging to be set free. Matthew is out of the car and racing at the woman before I can say anything. I hear him cry out as I am getting out of the car while trying to stay down. My fire is covering my hands, reaching in the direction I last saw her as I creep toward the back of the car. I am nearly there when the woman steps out from in front of the car. I throw my hands up to shield myself and the fire in my hands flares, intense heat and light scalding the very air. The roar of the flames is deafening. I try to lean away from the heat. It feels like I'm roasting. How do I shut this off? Fuck! What is that smell? It finally occurs to me to close my hands. It feels like the flames are fighting me about it, but I manage it, closing my hands and stopping the flames. When I open my eyes, I see the woman, or what's left of her. My empty stomach sends everything not in it up violently.

The dry heaves subside, and I carefully straighten, making sure I don't look at... her. Rounding the backside of the car, I see Matthew laying in the street unmoving. Oh no. No, no, no. Running over to him, I am kneeling at his side with my ear pressed to his chest when I hear the sirens approaching. He seems to be breathing. There is a lady burnt to death next to the exploded car. The car has to catch fire too. I run over; the sirens growing louder by the second. Reaching in, I grab my purse and then run to the front of the car. Focus, Blaze. You can do this. I tell the flames that they need to start with following the path of the explosion and then let the fire do its thing. It isn't exactly the best way to do this, but I don't know enough about this and the officials are nearly here. The flames start doing their thing, rushing in through the hole she blew in the radiator. I leave them to it and run to be on the pavement next to Matthew when they get here. I'm sticking as close to the truth as possible. Fuck me. "Matthew, Matthew, wake up! I need you! Don't make me do this alone."

His eyelids flutter and he shoots upright, shouting, "Blaze!" His hands stretched out toward the fire as he starts to get to his feet.

I grab his arm before he can stand. He jumps and swings, stopping himself as I shout, "It's me!"

I am near crushed in his arms as he pulls me onto his lap. The fire trucks and police screech to a stop. The world is noise and lights and people running around trying to put out the fire. Remembering the glamour that Glenda taught me, I run my hands over his head and create what will seem a very realistic knot on Matthew's forehead. Whispering to him about what I've done and what I plan for our story, I stop when a familiar voice says, "Excuse me, I'm officer Chad, I have some questions for you all. If you could come over here with me?"

I turn and look up into the face of my brother. Well, that should make things easier. "Blaze! What are you doing here?"

I shrug. "Getting attacked by strange women?"

"Is he ok? Matthew, are you ok?" He turns off his body cam as he kneels to get a better look.

"I put that there. It's just a glamour. The lady beside the car attacked us. But I, I was the one that set… that set, um… everything on fire." I swallow to force down the lump in my throat from even thinking about it.

"Fuck. There's a dead woman next to the car? And she burnt to death? How did the car get blown to shit?"

"She did that. I just made it all catch fire. She knocked Matthew out, but he heals so fast…"

"Yeah, yeah. Ok. So, luckily, the fire investigator is one of us. I'll tell him the actual story and the fake one."

"Define one of us. She was a witch."

"He's a cousin. What the hell? Why are witches attacking you?"

"I'll explain later. I have a lot to tell you."

"You damn well do. What the fuck is going on here?"

"Can we talk about it tonight, at Dad's place?"

He looks around, "Yeah. Let's get the two of you up and out of here."

AUTHOR'S NOTE

Well that was a ride. Blaze and Matthew took this story to places I didn't expect and I hope you enjoyed the ride as much as I did. I hope to get A Dream of Wolves up for preorder shortly. That and Olivia's Prison. If you haven't read Olivia's Fall yet, now is the time. I will be writing Olivia's Prison next.

Curious about Blaze's mom and how she became so

beaten down? Her story is coming, but it is going to my newsletter people first. Subscribe here: rhiannon-futch.ck. page/back-matter

I have some of my socials linked in the about author page, would love to see you there. Until then, happy reading!

Rhiannon

Rhiannon Futch is a paranormal romance author and Chaos Coordinator, tarot deck collector, rescue dog mom, and craft enthusiast. She has been published since 2019 and is happily settled into writing vampire smut.

Record screech noise here Until the 2024 election she was happily settled into the one genre. Now she is also writing feminist horror novellas, blending her feminism with a dark nature and an immense well of feminine rage.

Wolfie, She-ra, and Daemon are her fully spoiled doggos who live for outdoor games and treat time. She is a night owl with a deep love of fall and winter and teaches yoga to authors but has never managed a headstand.

She is rarely found out in the world, preferring deep woods in the winter and cool writing spaces during the summer. Rhiannon lives in eastern North Carolina currently, with hopes of returning to the mountains of western North Carolina.

If you would like to see what books are next or sign up for her newsletter, visit rhiannonfutchauthor.com (You get a free book when you sign up!) You can also use the QR code (on the next page) to get to my website.

Mercy of the Vampire King

Shame of the Vampire King

Pursuit of the Vampire King

Prey of the Vampire King

Reign of the Vampire King

Love and Vampires Series

Olivia's Fall

Olivia's Prison

Olivia's Flight

Olivia's Family

Warriors of the Old Gods series

A Dream of Wolves

A Dream of Stone

A Dream of Ravens

A Dream of Bones

Her Violent Silence novella series

Wolf Goddess

Coyote Offerings

Old Wolf Woman

Witches Reclaimed series

Titles TBD